we are breathing

Making comics has influenced the course of my life and the way I think about the world more profoundly than I could ever describe. Thanks to Box Brown, Frank Santoro, L. Nichols, and Kevin Czap, all of whom have published my work in beautiful print editions. Thanks to Kimball Anderson, Derik Badman, and Warren Craghead, the collaborators who graciously allowed their work to be reprinted here. Thanks to Alec Bery for conducting a thoughtful and flattering interview. Thanks to my friends in comics, who have shown me the way: Madeleine, Juan, Sal, Simon, Oliver, those already mentioned above, and so many more. Thanks to CEM, who was here for the creation of all of these stories and who has a much better eye for color and layout than I'll ever have.

"Untitled" (with Derik Badman) originally appeared in Rebus. "Ripples" originally appeared In Ink Brick: A Journal of Comics Poetry No. 8. Many of the other comics in this collection originally appeared in self-published editions.

Visit whitecomics.co.

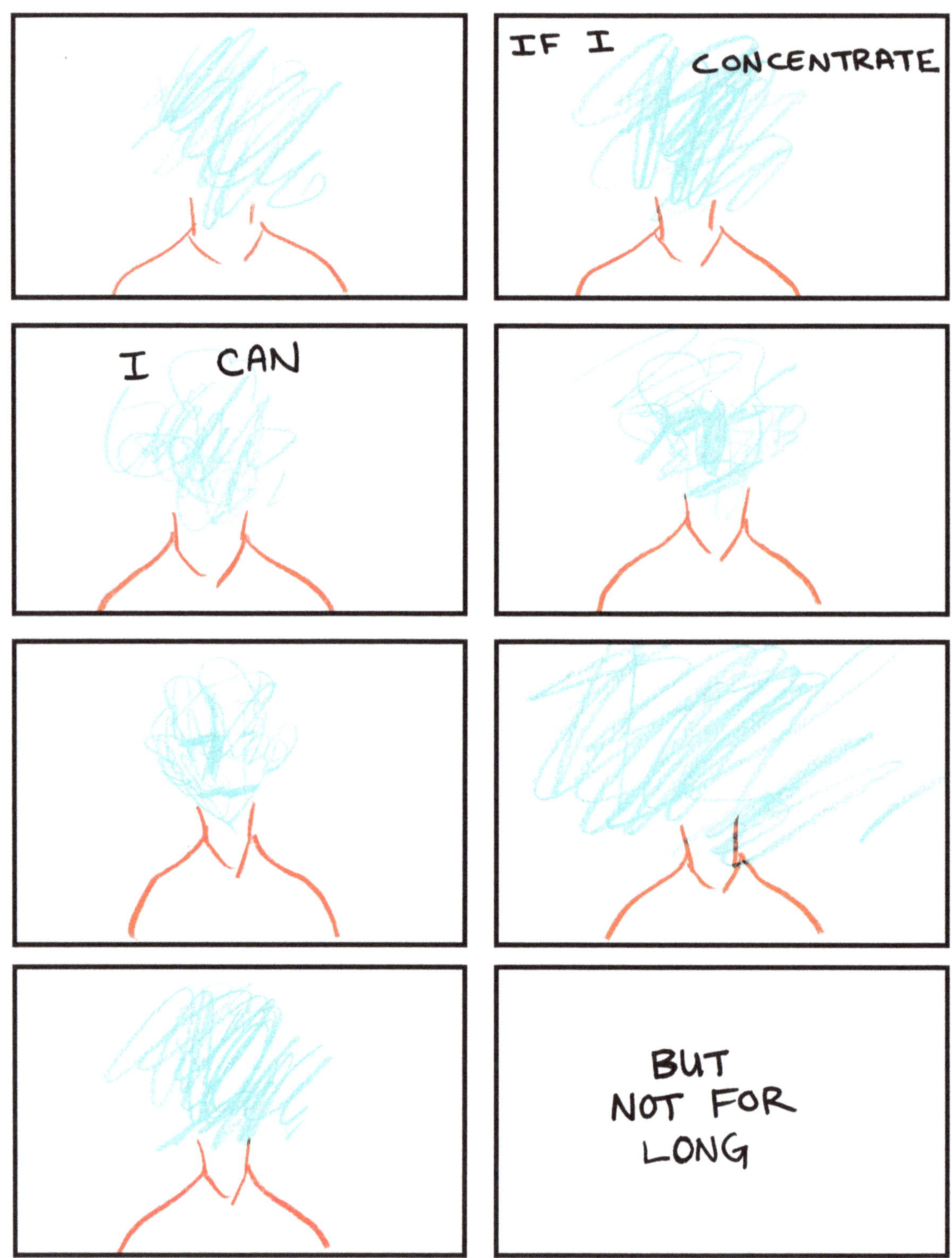

IF I
CONCENTRATE
I CAN
BUT
NOT FOR
LONG

table of contents

YOU ARE HERE

[THE SOUND OF THE WIND, WHISTLING SOFTLY AND BLOWING SPECKS OF DUST INTO YOUR EYES THAT YOU BLINK AWAY. YOU MAY WHISTLE OUT LOUD IF IT HELPS YOU TO IMAGINE THIS.]

IN FRONT OF YOU IS

BEHIND YOU IS

[THE WIND CONTINUES TO BLOW, CHANGING PITCH IN A WAY THAT WOULD BE MELODIOUS IF IT WASN'T SO SINISTER.]

YOU LOOK DOWN AT YOUR HANDS, CRACKED AND DRY.

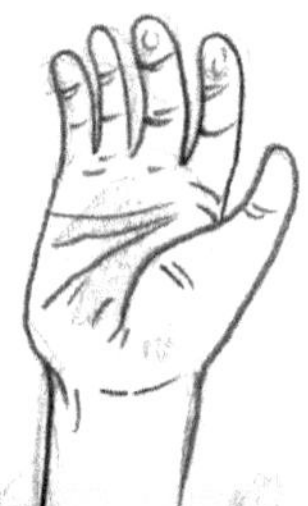

OW, THAT HURT. YOU HOPE YOU WILL FIND WATER SOON.

[THE WIND DIES DOWN, ENGULFING YOU SUDDENLY IN A STILL SILENCE. STOP WHISTLING. YOU'RE STARTING TO BOTHER THE NEIGHBORS.]

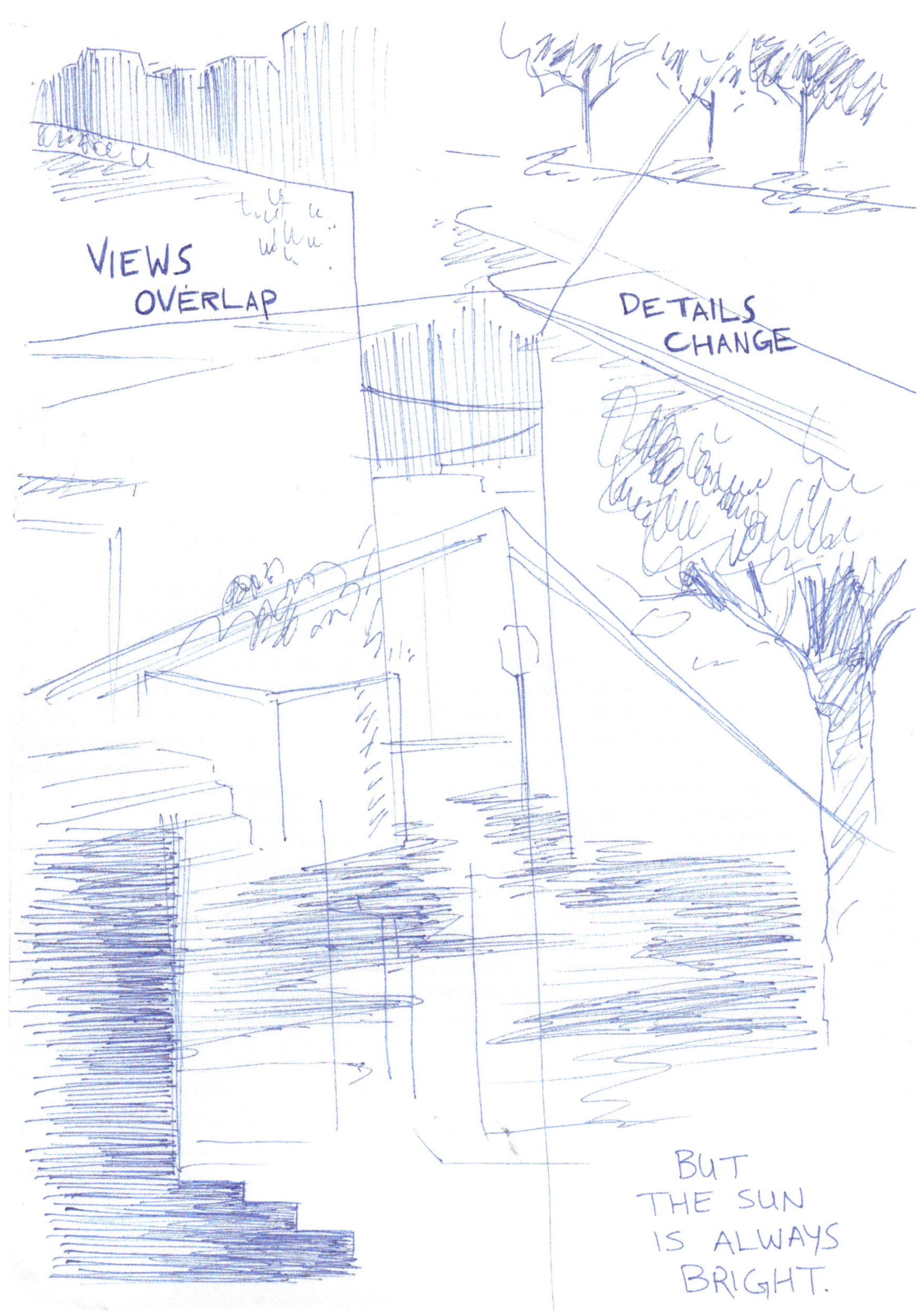

VIEWS OVERLAP
DETAILS CHANGE
BUT THE SUN IS ALWAYS BRIGHT.

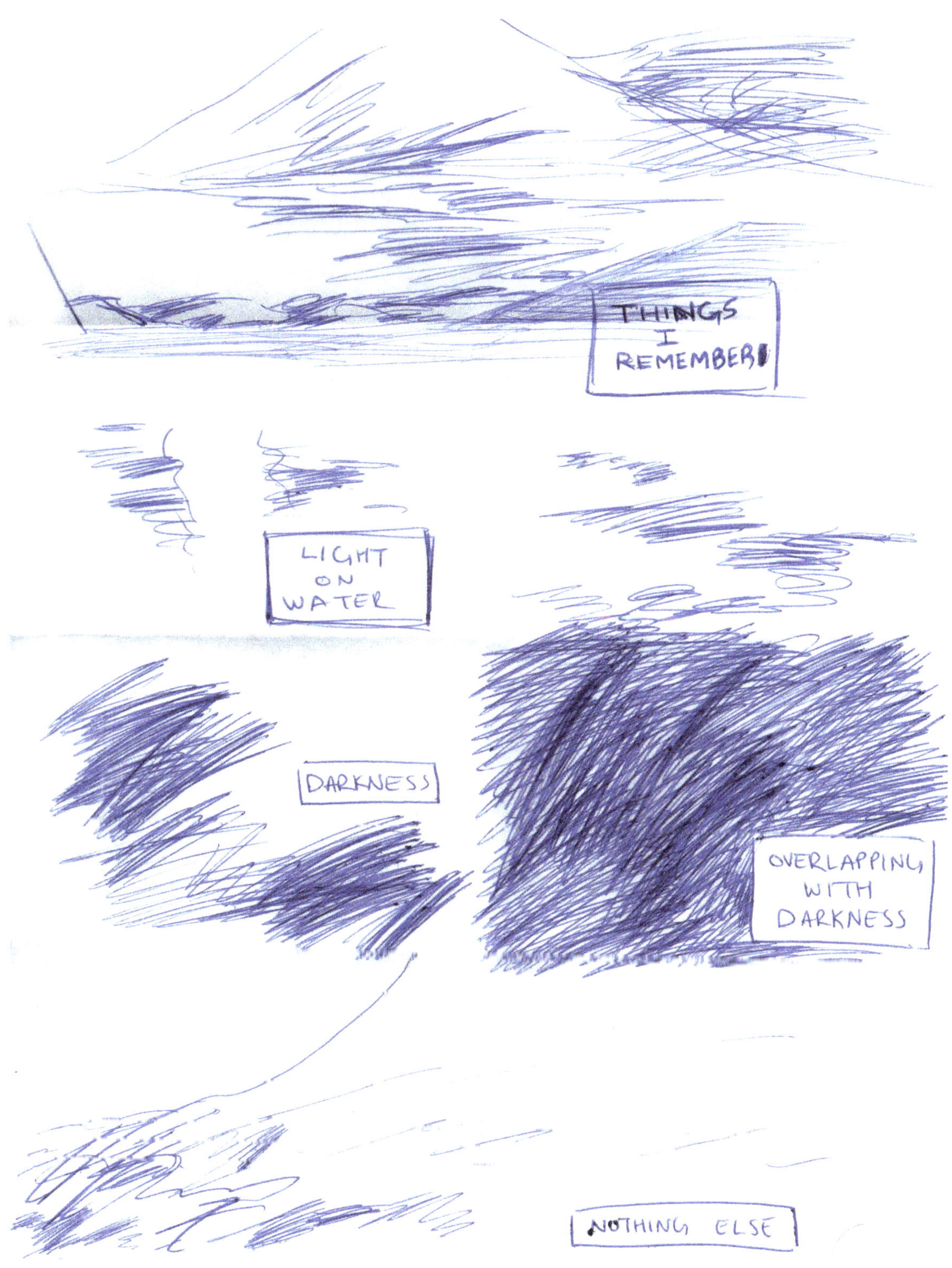
THINGS
I
REMEMBER
LIGHT
ON
WATER
DARKNESS
OVERLAPPING
WITH
DARKNESS
NOTHING ELSE

march

MOST HIGH
MOST MIGHTY

MOST PUISSANT
CAE SAR

METELLUS CIMBER THROWS
BEFORE THY SEAT

AN HUMBLE HE ART

No.

The
thing

that disturbs
me most as
we wait

is just seeing
that it's a
beautiful
March day.

All is
calm.

I MUST PREVENT THEE CIMBER
THESE LOWLY COURTESIES
MIGHT FIRE THE BLOOD OF ORDINARY MEN
BE NOT FOND TO THINK
THAT CAES

DOTH NOT

BRUTUS

BOOTLESS KNEEL?

GREAT CAESAR

HENCE

WILT THOU LIFT UP OLYMPUS?

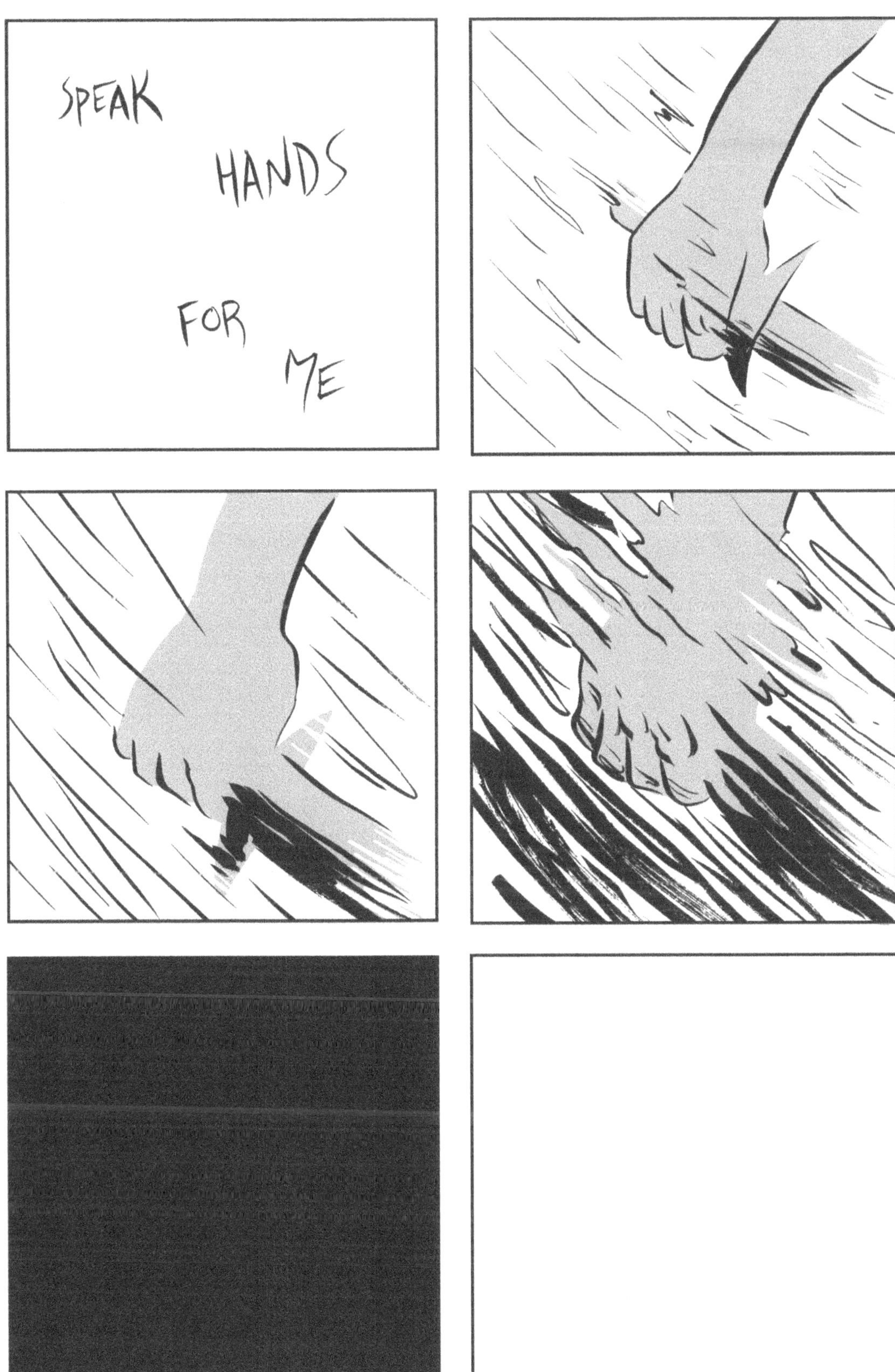

SPEAK
HANDS
FOR
ME

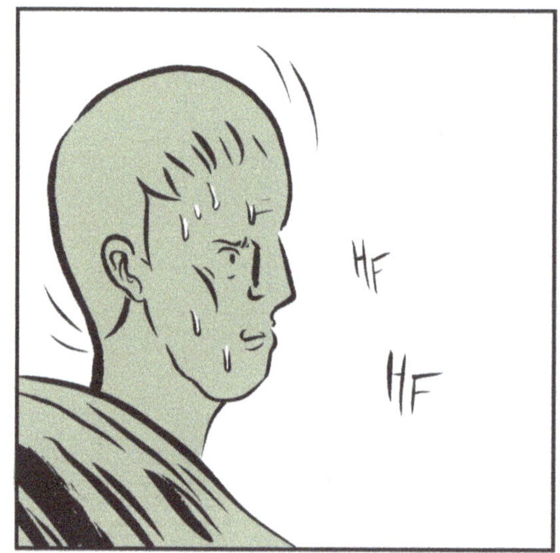
HF
HF

Shake
Shake

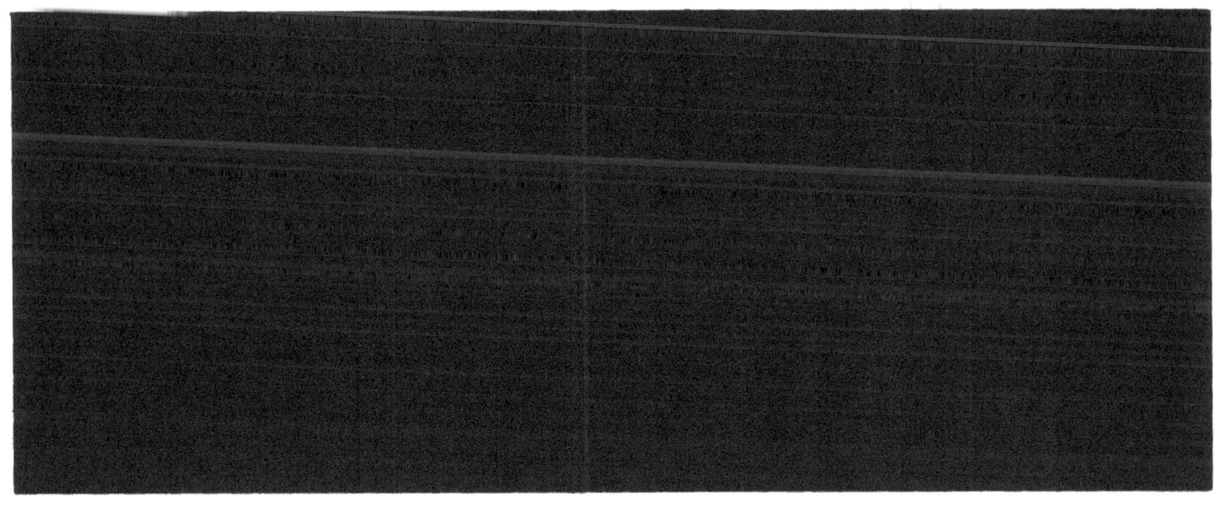

BLACK
PILLARS

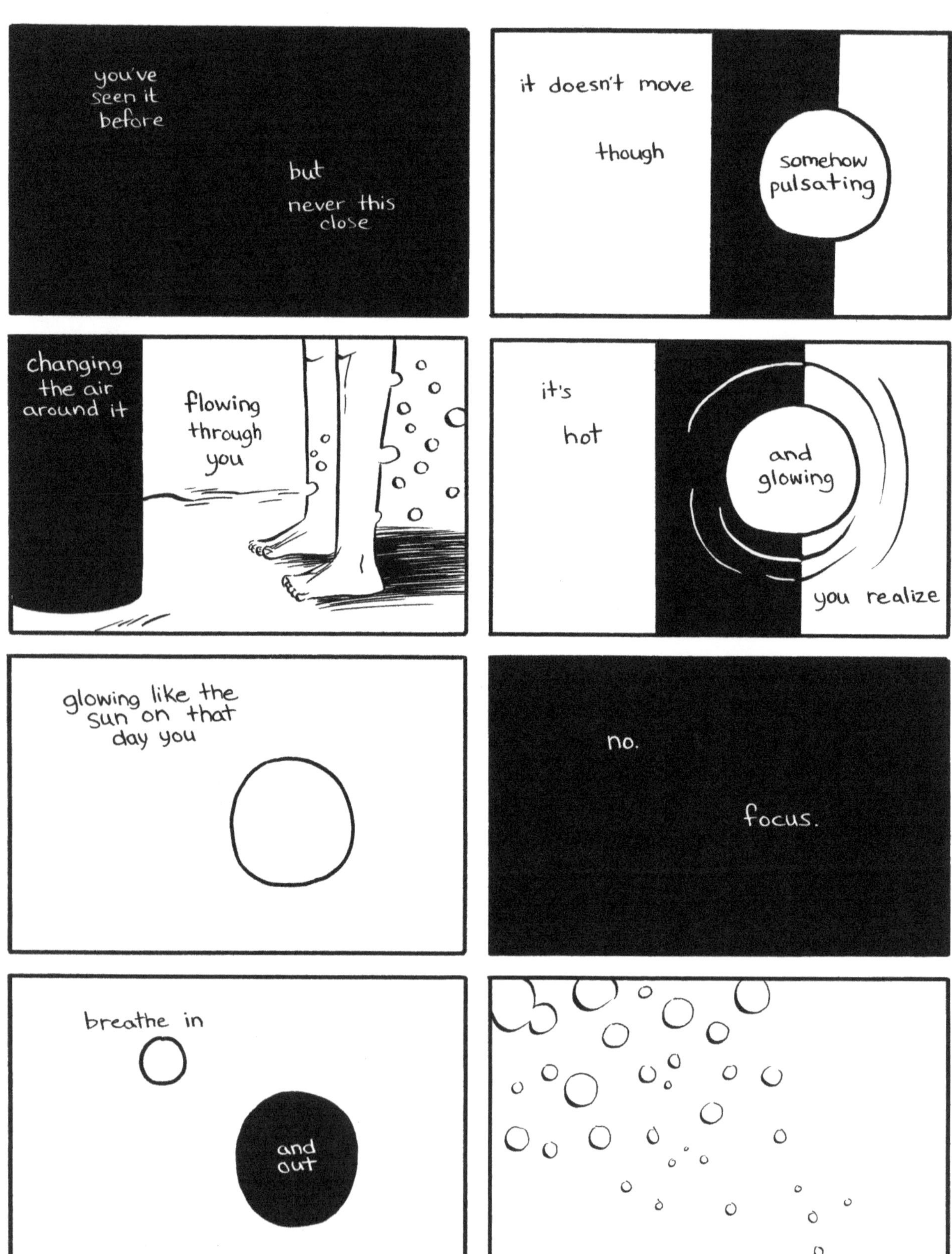
you've
seen it
before

but
never this
close

it doesn't move

though

somehow
pulsating

changing
the air
around it

flowing
through
you

it's

hot

and
glowing

you realize

glowing like the
sun on that
day you

no.

focus.

breathe in

and
out

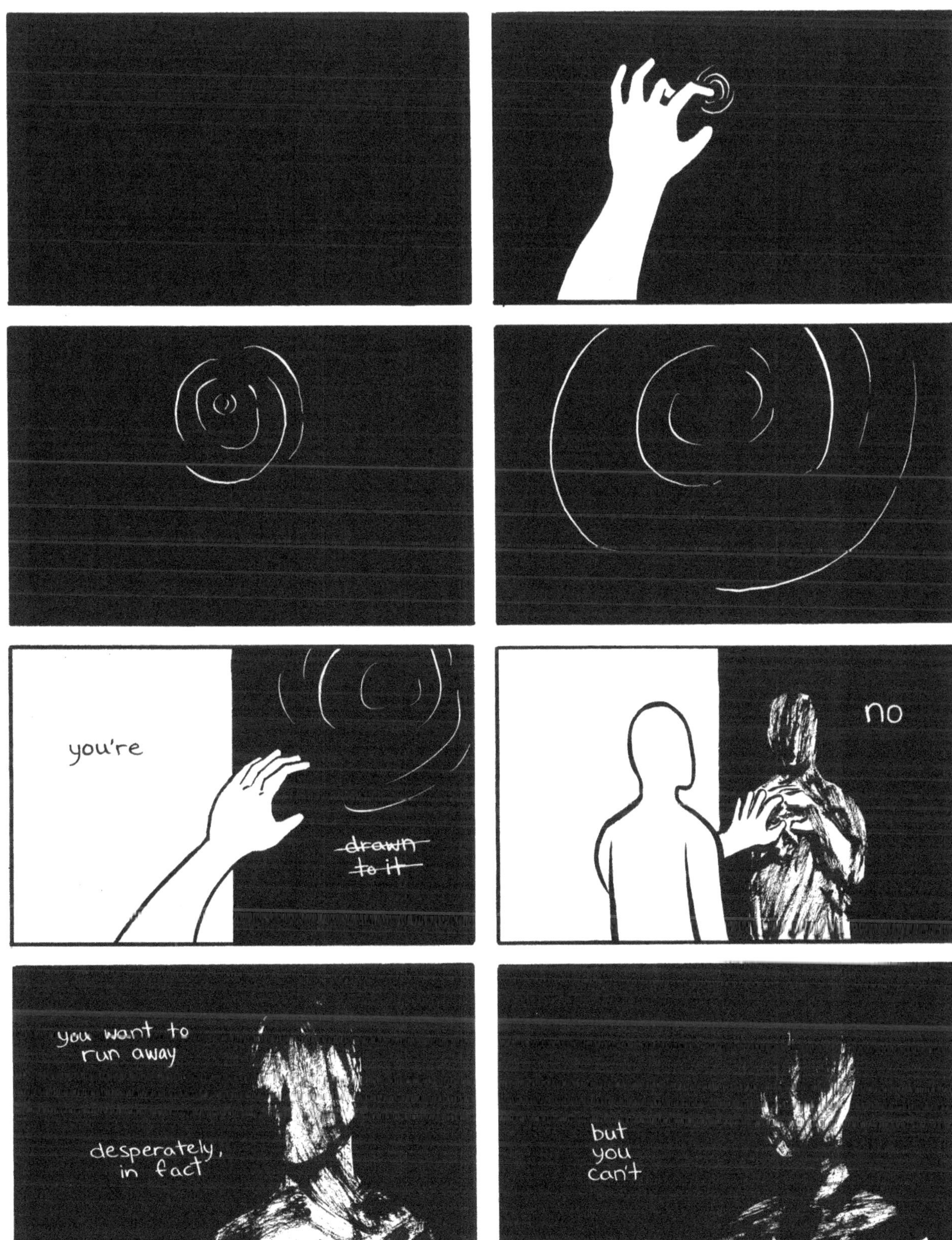

you're
drawn
to it
no
you want to
run away
desperately,
in fact
but
you
can't

you look
up, then

you wonder
if they can
see you
but you know
they can see
the pillar

does it
ever end?
you
wonder

could someone
be looking down
on the pillar

the same
way the plane
looks down
on you now?

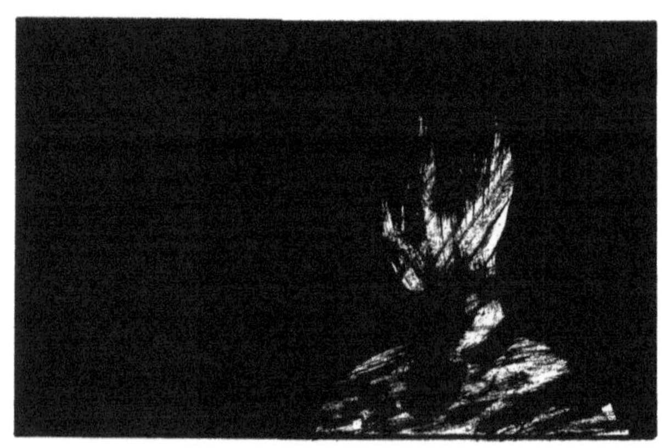

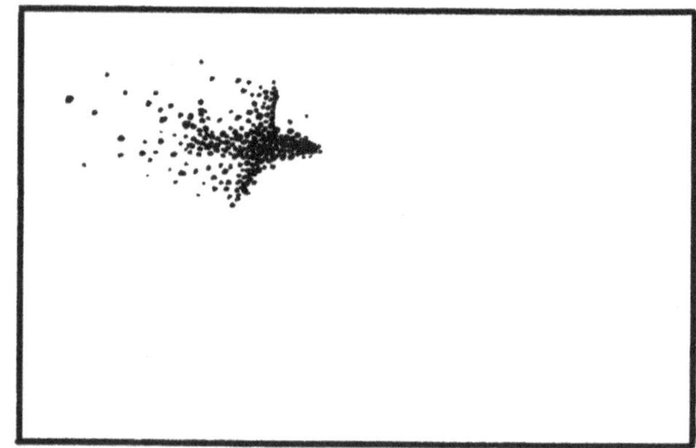

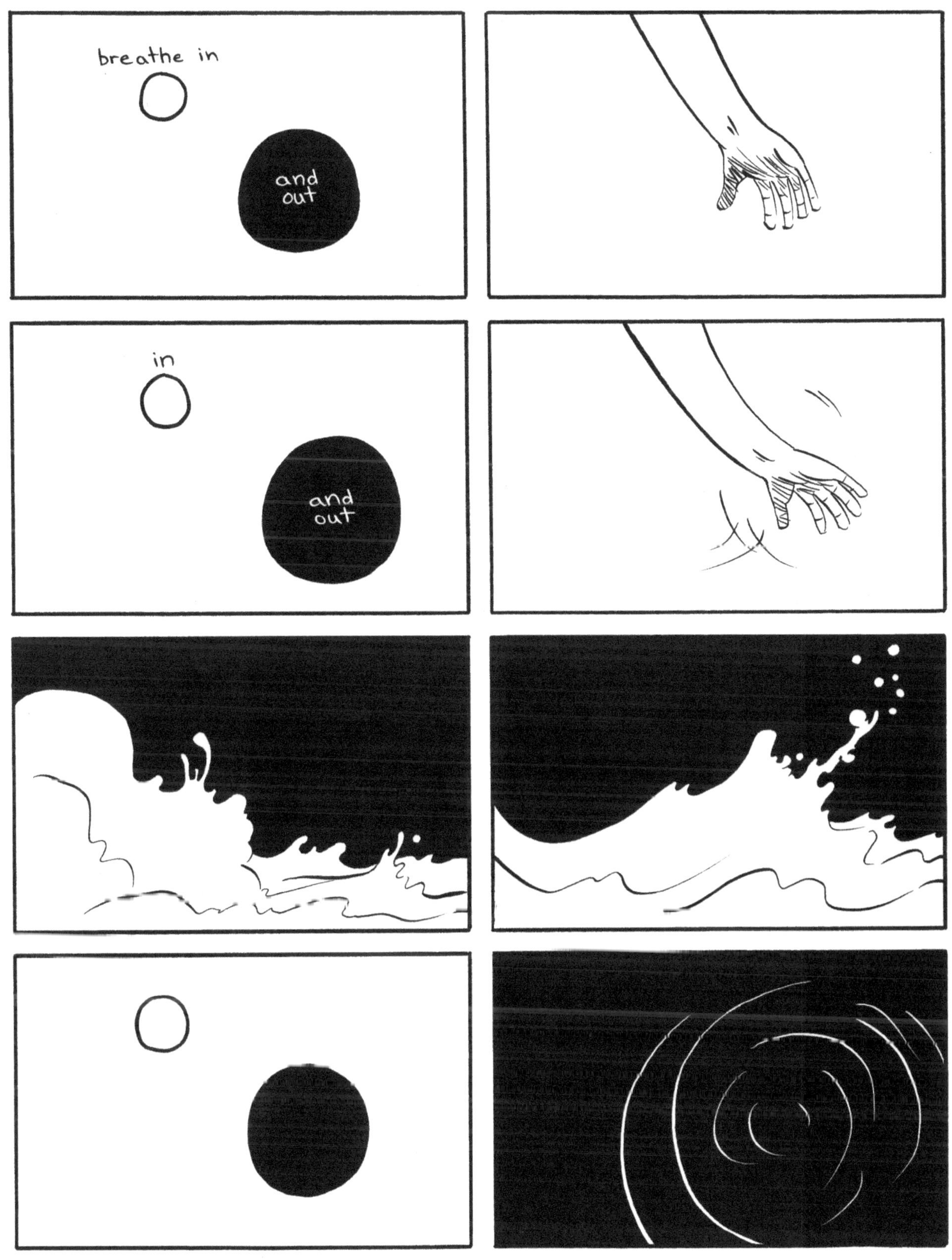

breathe in
and out
in
and out
breathe in

you imagine your hand on the other side
try
to move your fingers
you can't feel them, you realize
but you know they're still there
they must be

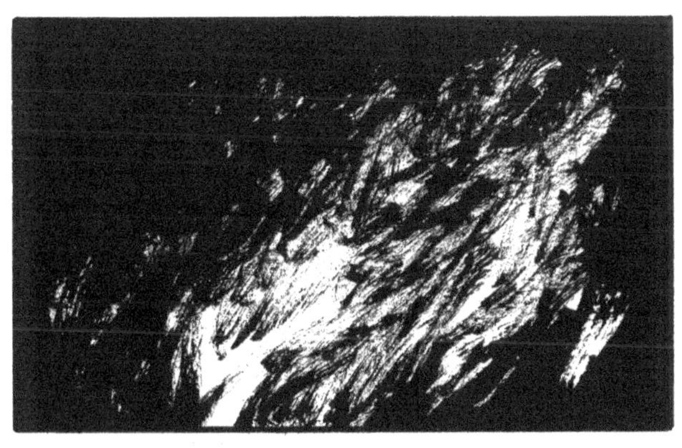

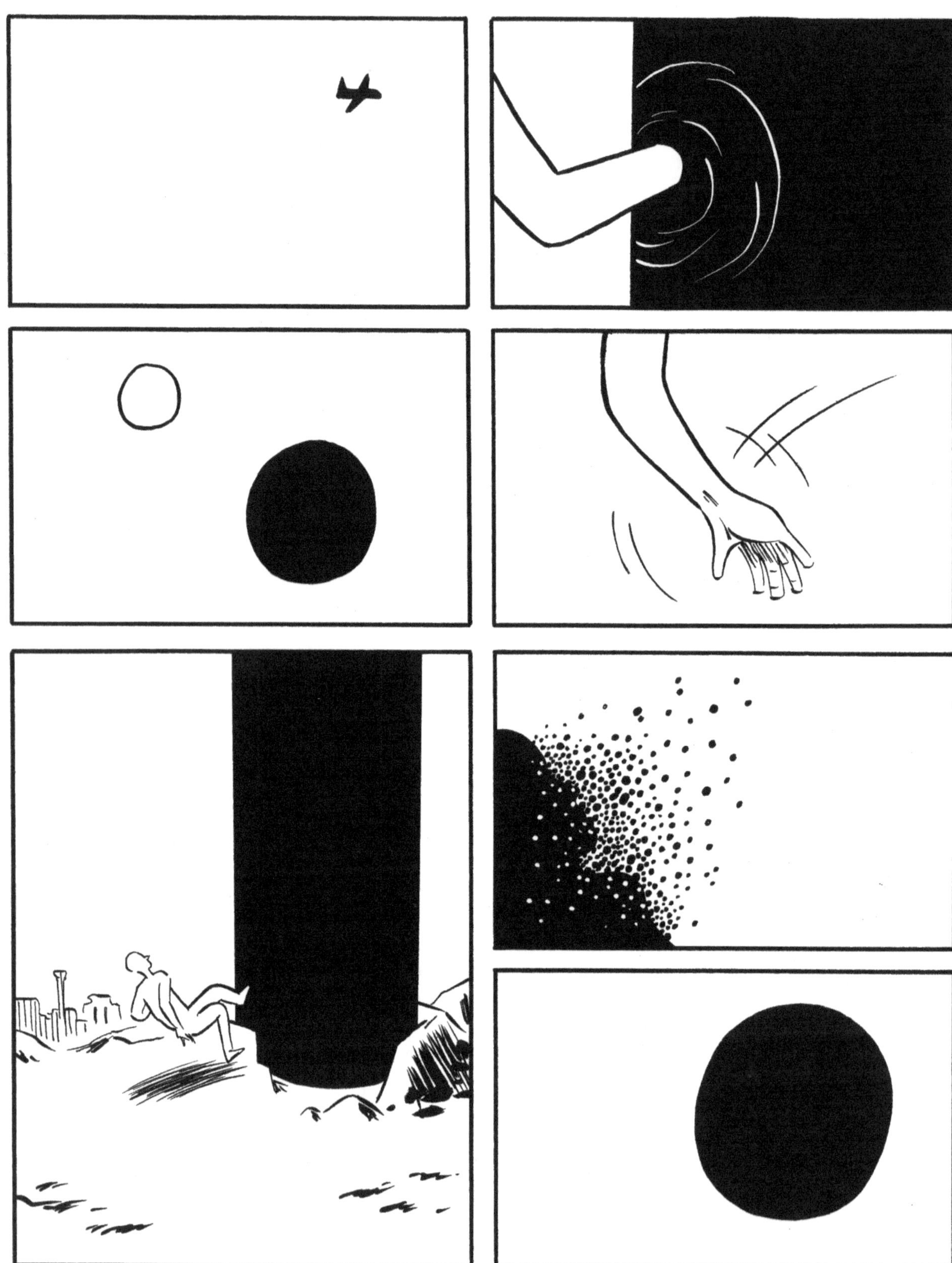

PAWN
I NEVER KEEP MY EYES ON THE ROAD
I MEAN, I'LL LOOK AT IT OCCASIONALLY
BUT
I DON'T KNOW.
I CAN'T EXPLAIN IT.
AND I DON'T NEED TO THINK RIGHT NOW.

EVERY DRIVE SEEMS LIKE ONE LONG TRIP
REMEMBERED DETAILS
INTERMINGLING WITH WHAT SEEMS TO BE THE PRESENT
THOUGH I CAN NEVER REALLY BE SURE

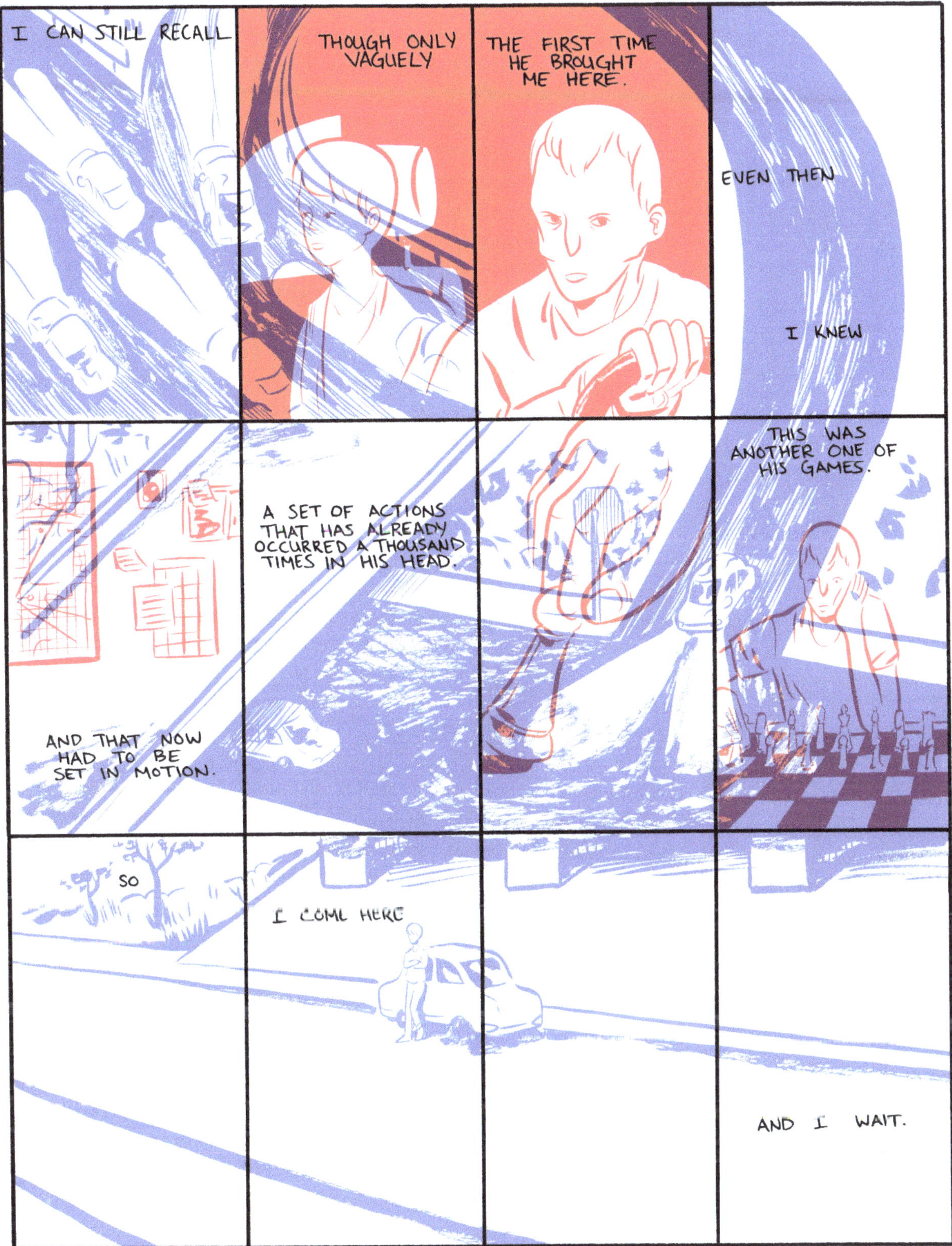

I CAN STILL RECALL
THOUGH ONLY VAGUELY
THE FIRST TIME HE BROUGHT ME HERE.
EVEN THEN
I KNEW
A SET OF ACTIONS THAT HAS ALREADY OCCURRED A THOUSAND TIMES IN HIS HEAD.
AND THAT NOW HAD TO BE SET IN MOTION.
THIS WAS ANOTHER ONE OF HIS GAMES.
SO
I COME HERE
AND I WAIT.

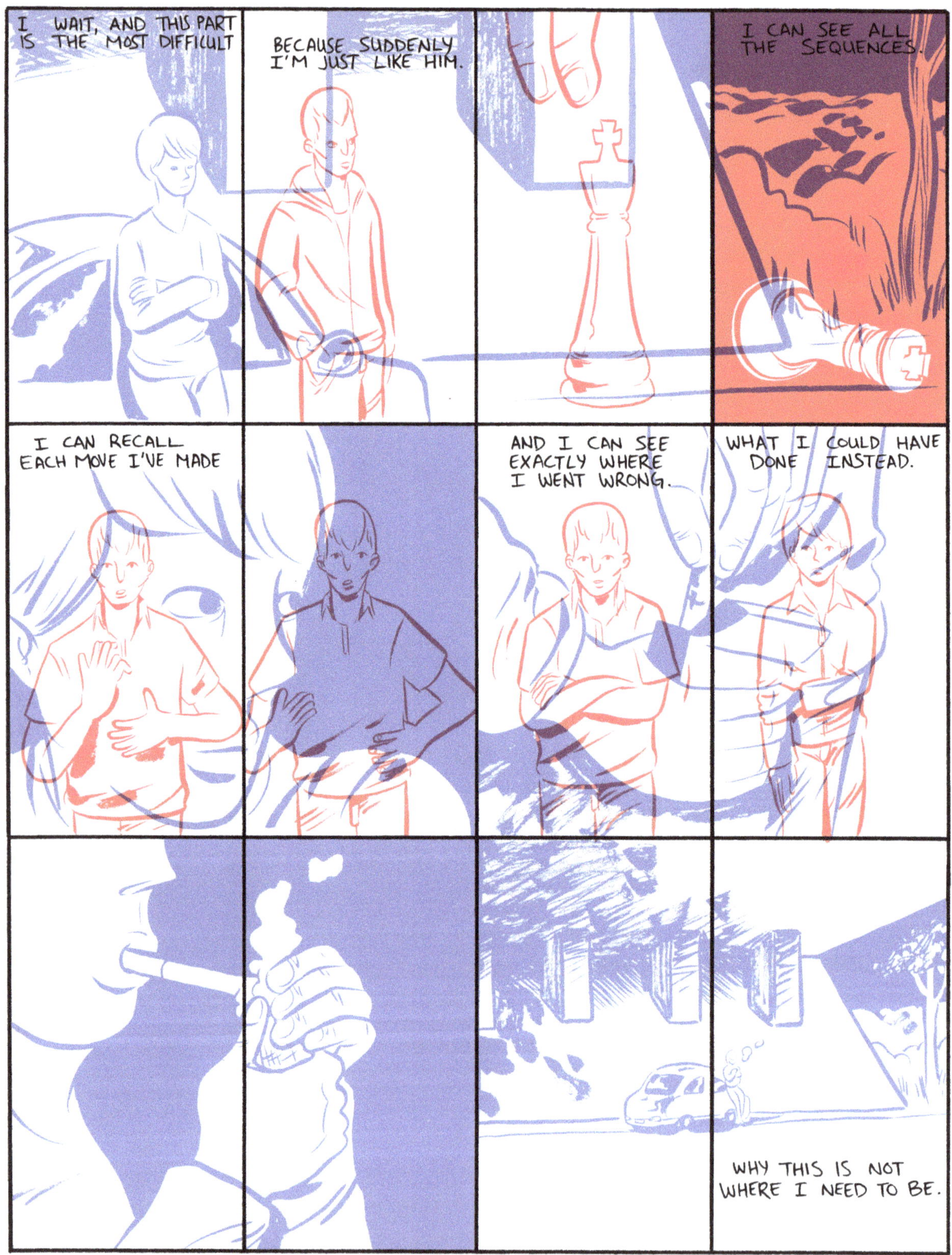

I WAIT, AND THIS PART IS THE MOST DIFFICULT
BECAUSE SUDDENLY I'M JUST LIKE HIM.
I CAN SEE ALL THE SEQUENCES.
I CAN RECALL EACH MOVE I'VE MADE
AND I CAN SEE EXACTLY WHERE I WENT WRONG.
WHAT I COULD HAVE DONE INSTEAD.
WHY THIS IS NOT WHERE I NEED TO BE.

BUT THEN
HE APPEARS
HOW WAS IT?
IT'S READY
LET'S GO HOME.

HE APPEARS
AND I REMEMBER
I REMEMBER THAT MY WORLD OF AIR AND SOIL
IS NOT HIS WORLD OF GRIDS AND NUMBERS
I TAKE COMFORT IN THAT THOUGHT
AND I REMIND MYSELF THAT ONCE A MOVE HAS BEEN MADE
THE CLOCK CAN NEVER BE TURNED BACK.
W
MAR 13

WHILE A SOFT
FOG WANDERS

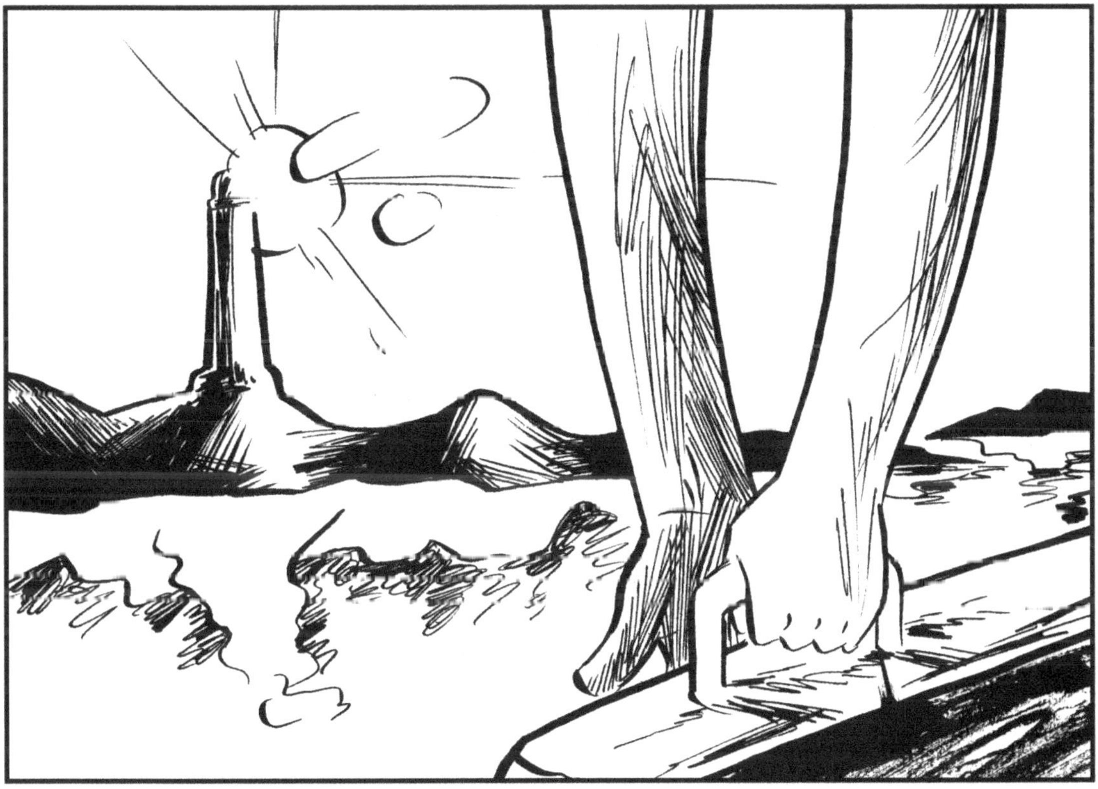

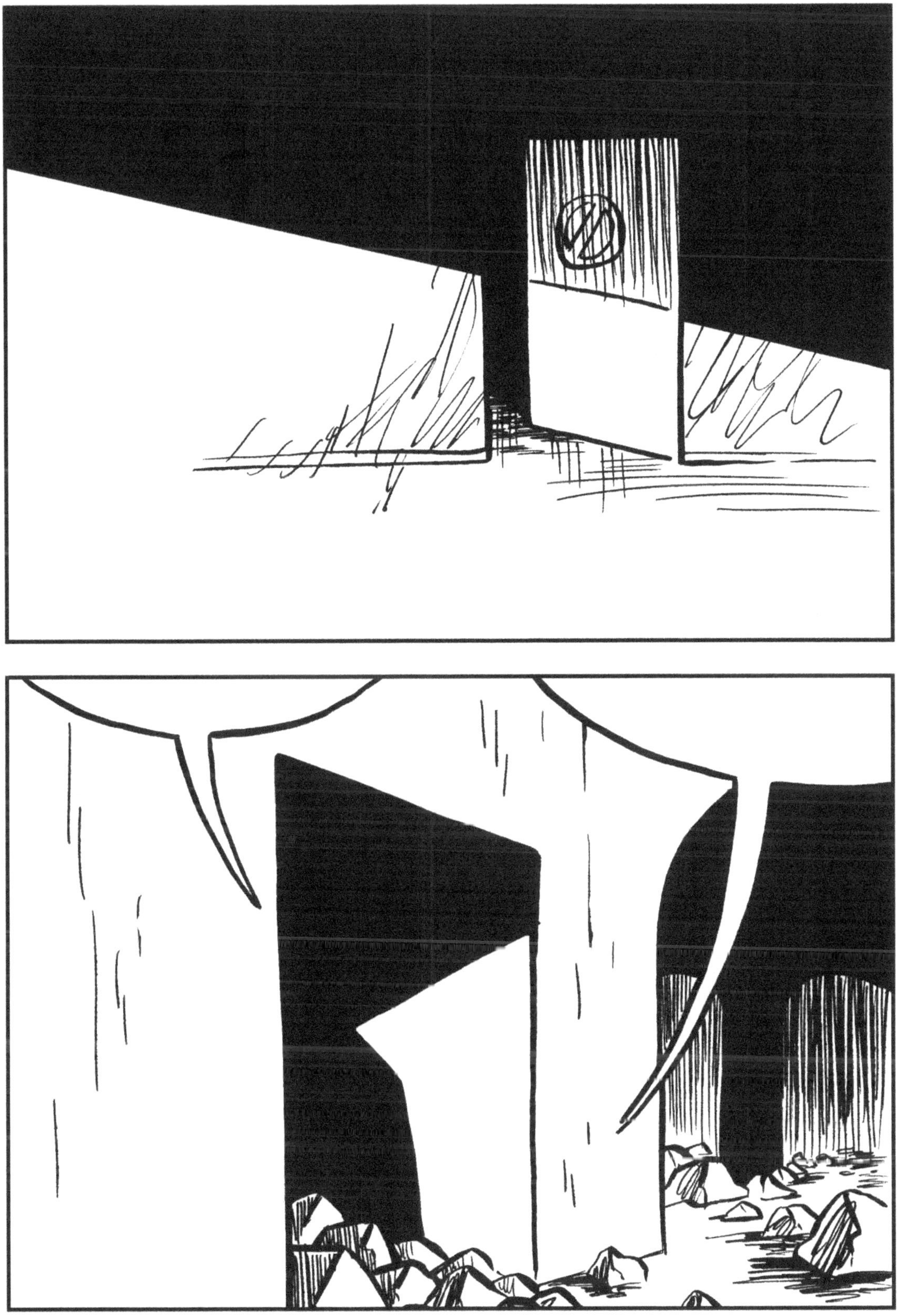

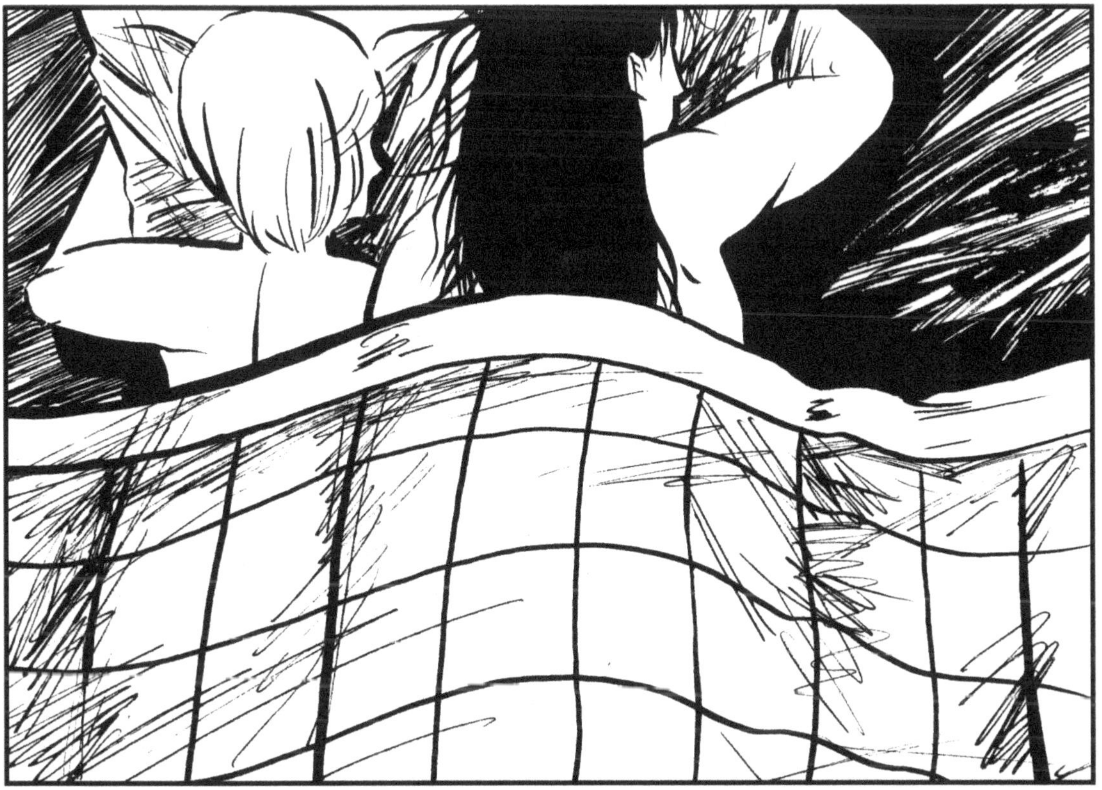

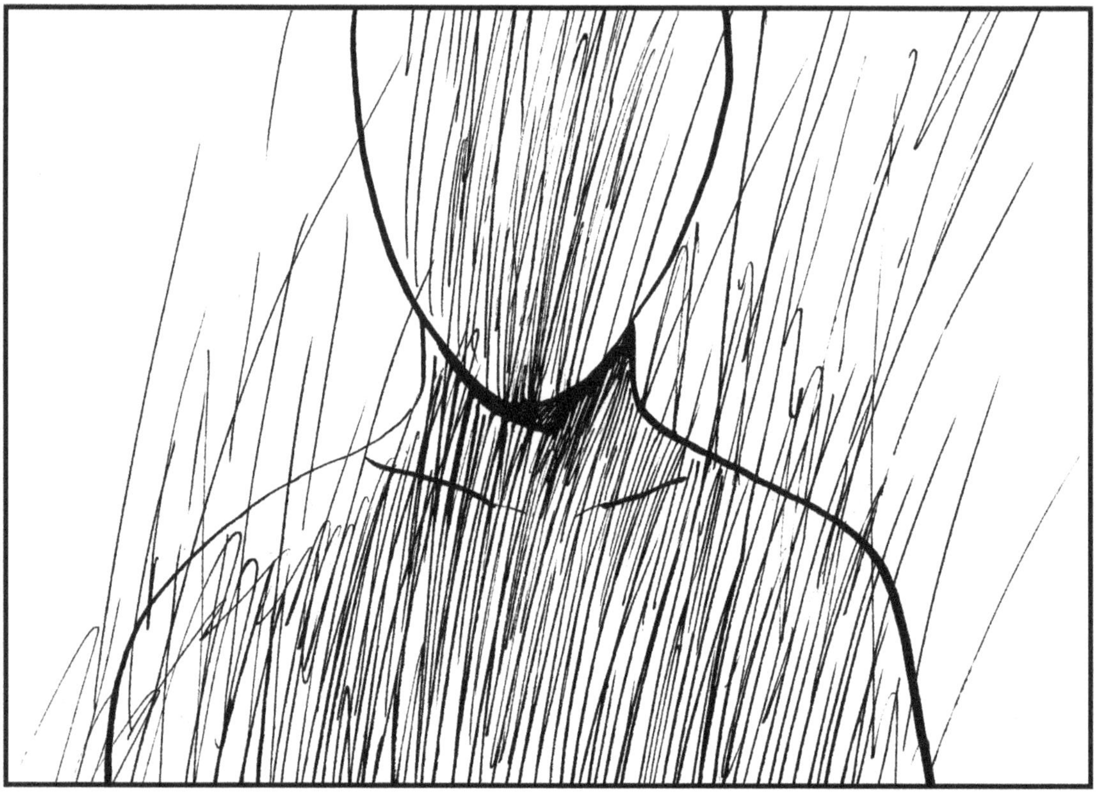

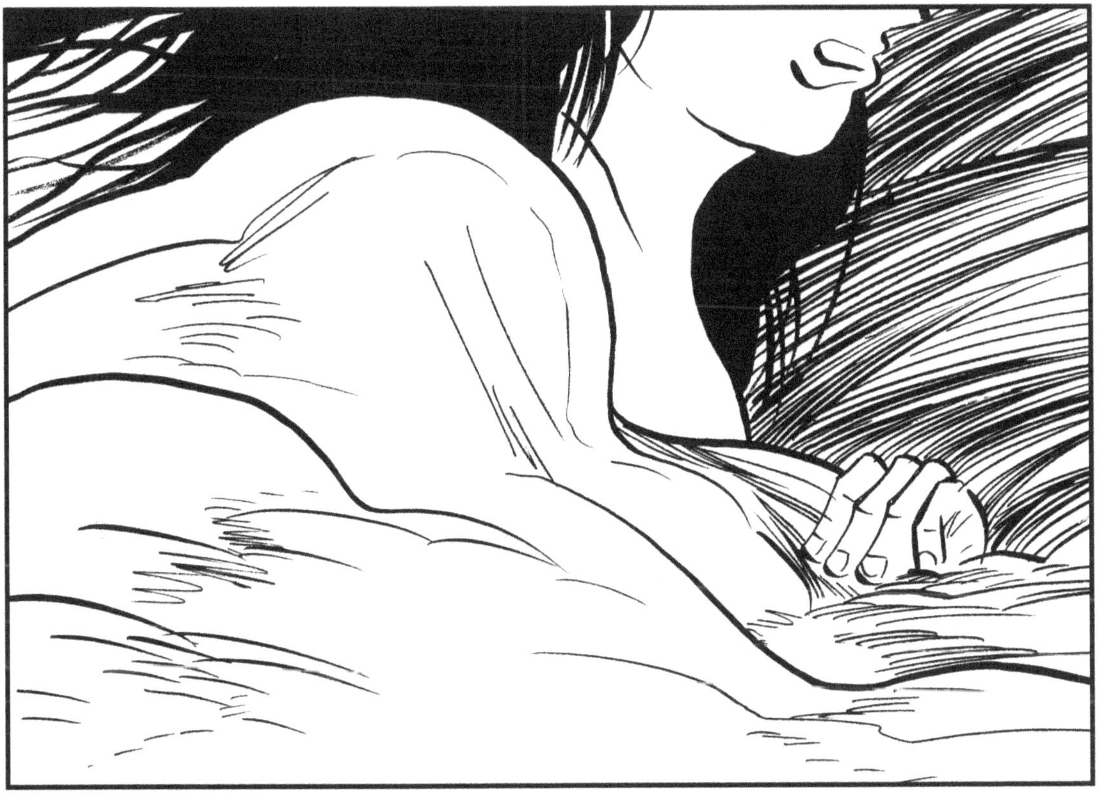

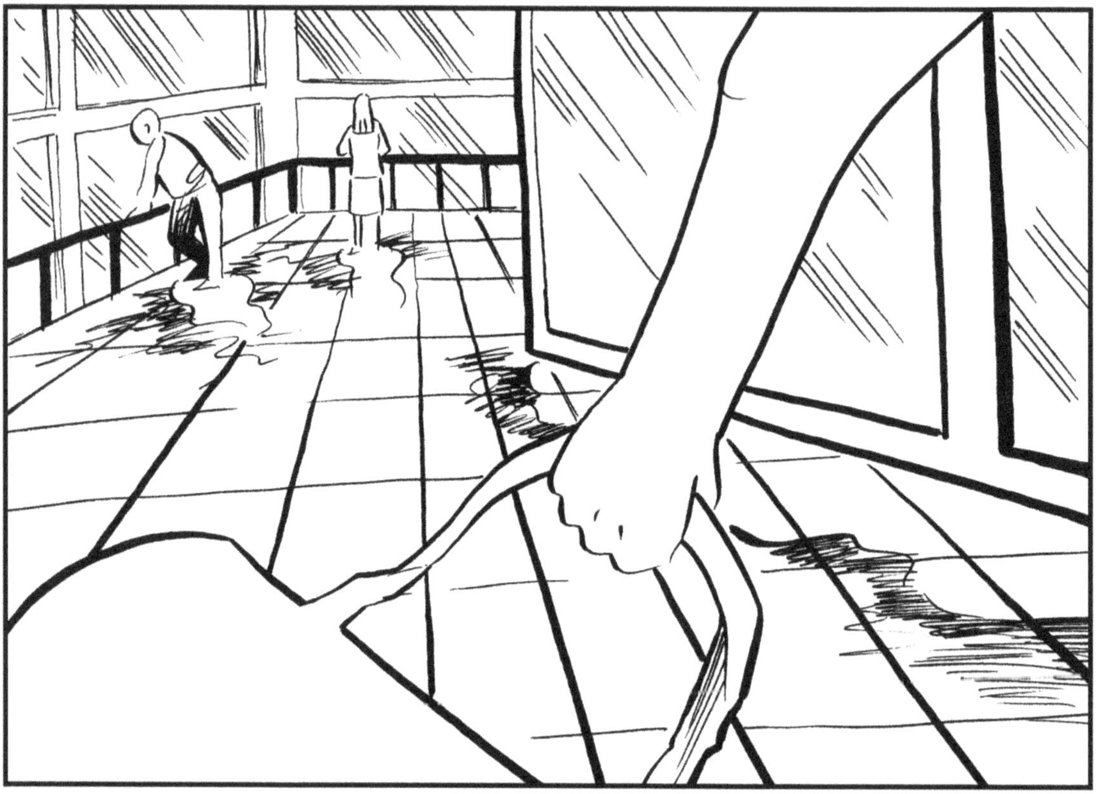

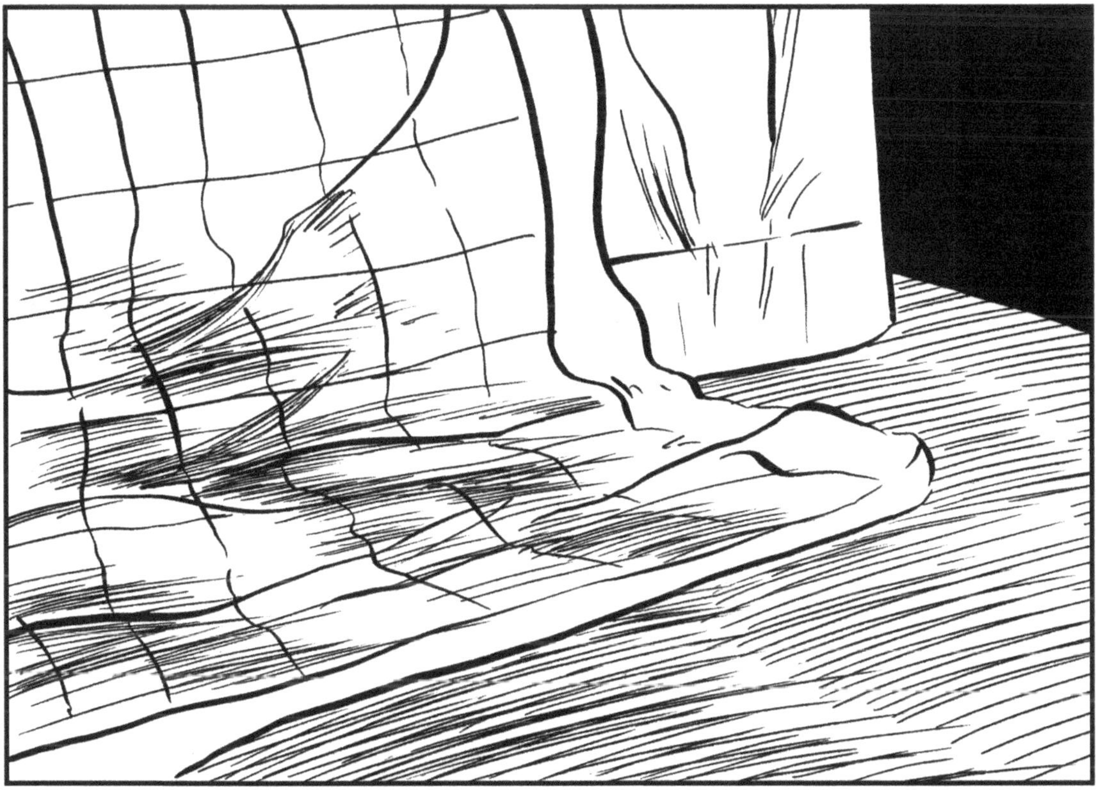

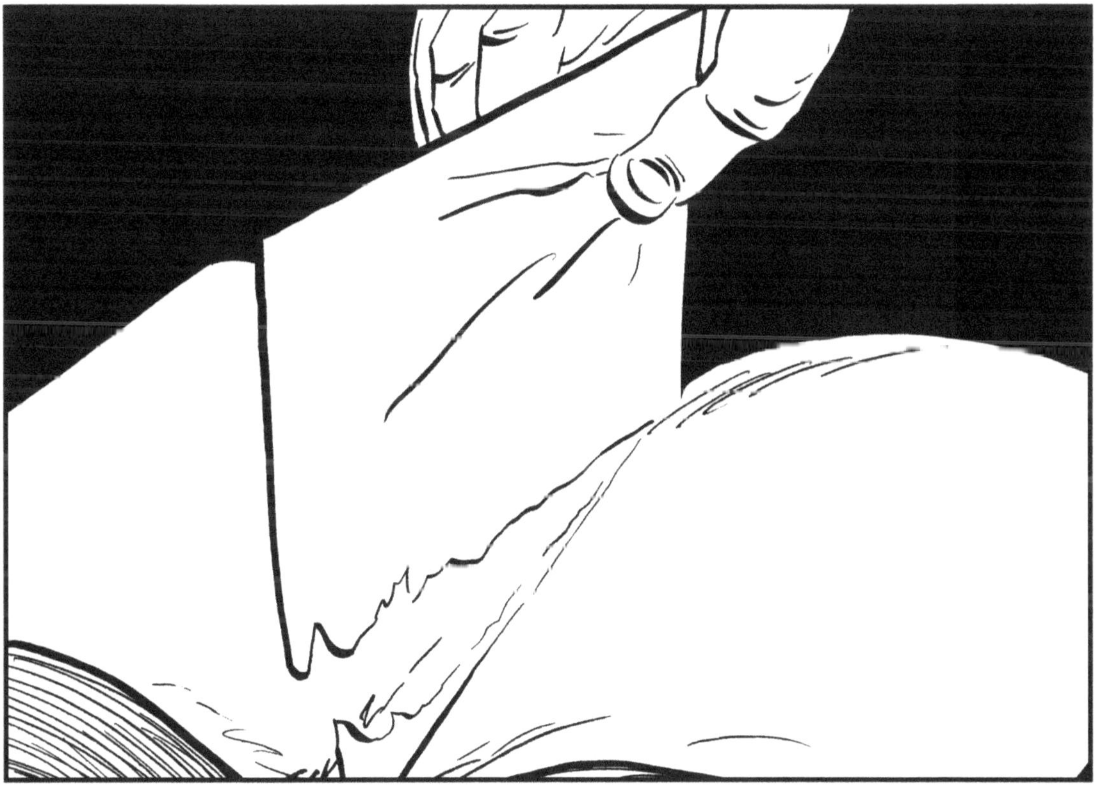

they have merely
painted layers

according to
dreamt up
a formula
late

look
substitute for something to hold on to

grasp at the everyday
but a tiny thoughts
fact that slip away

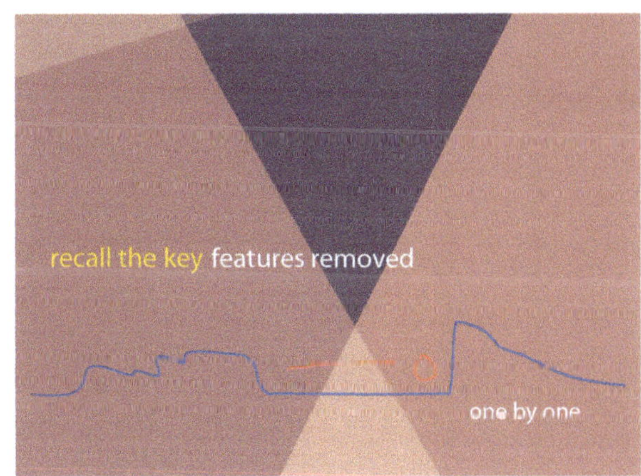
recall the key features removed
one by one

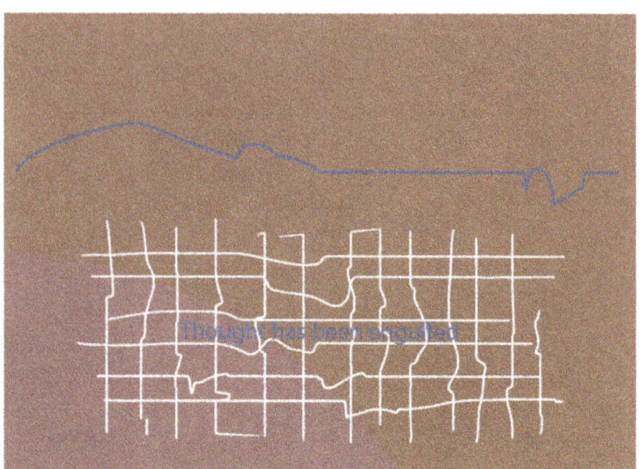

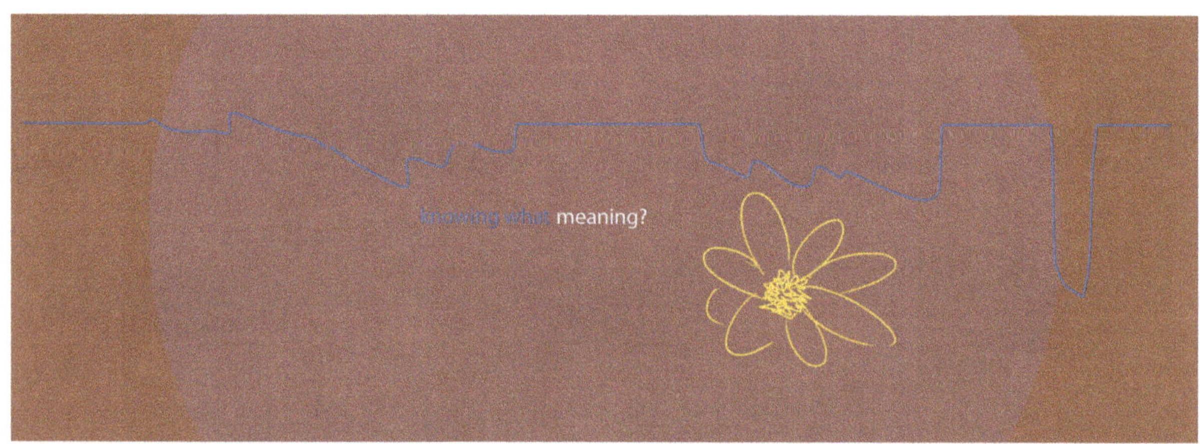

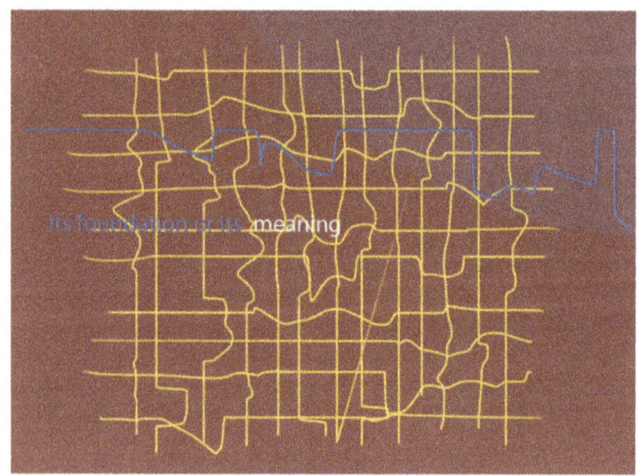

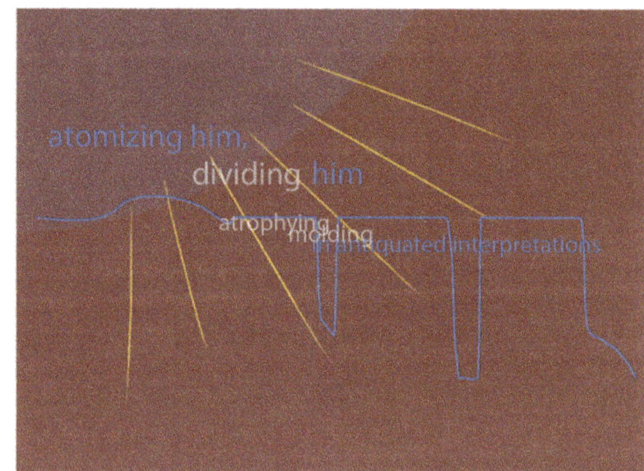

Andrew White + *Derik Badman*

CRACKLING

WHISTLING
SOFT SOUNDS

THOUGHTS

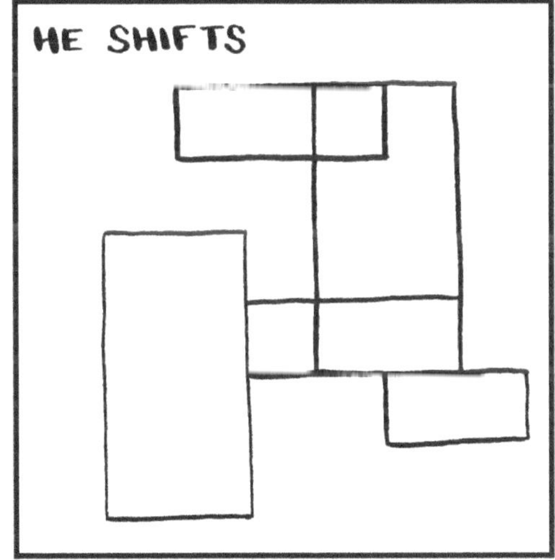
HE SHIFTS

DRIFTING

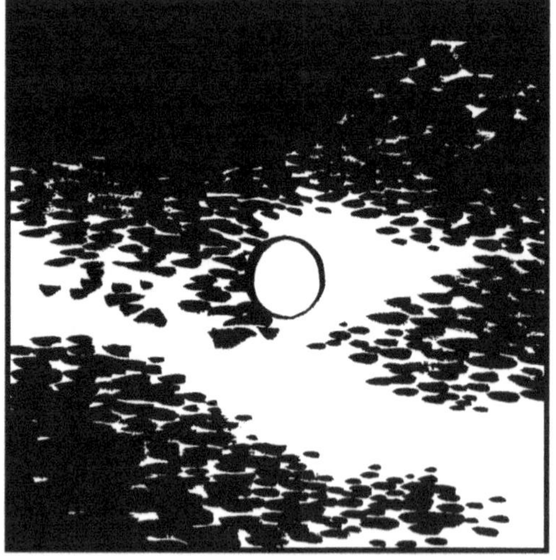

NO
THOUGHTS ROLL PLACCIDLY THROUGH HIS MIND

HE SHIFTS

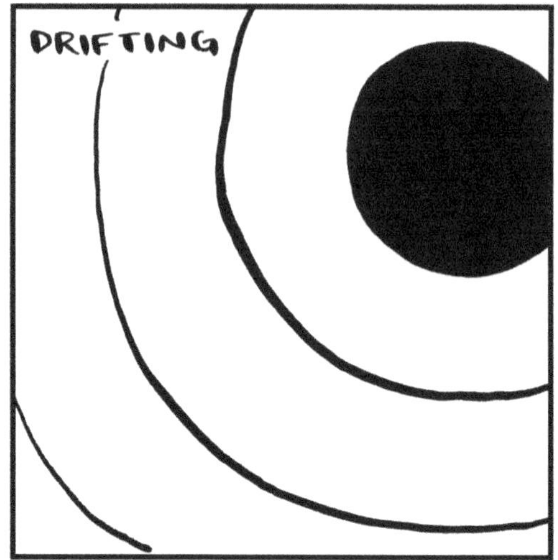
DRIFTING

BAD TIMING

THAT'S ALL IT IS

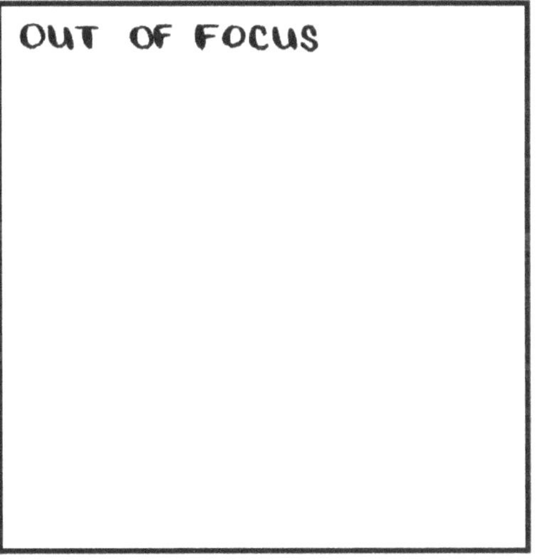
OUT OF FOCUS

NO
NO

THERE'S SOMETHING
TO BE REACHED

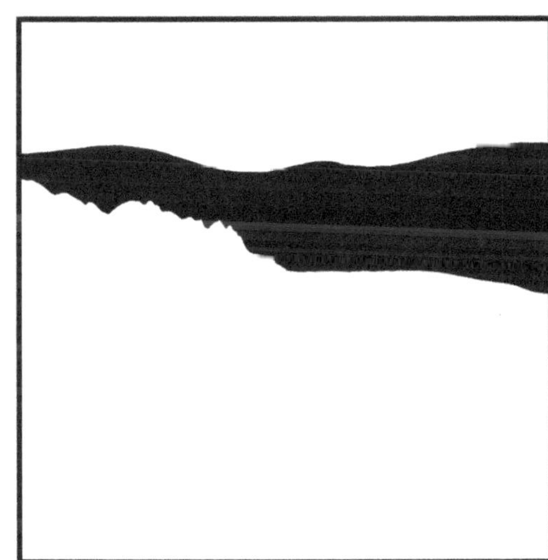

I CAN SEE IT

ANDREW WHITE, FEBRUARY 2014, BASED ON A COMIC GENERATED BY DERIK BADMAN

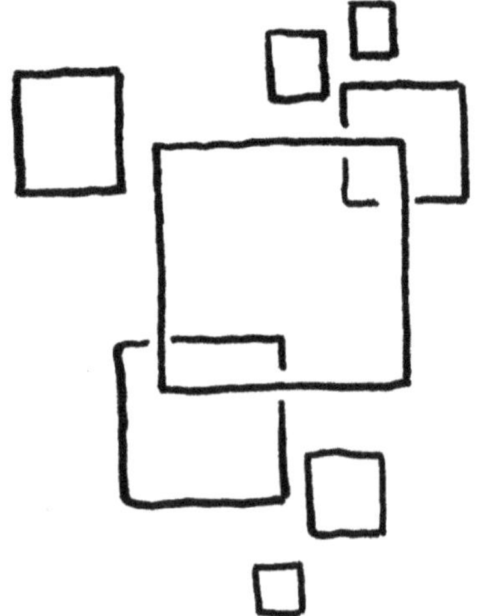

FILL'D
BASED ON A DRAWING BY WARREN CRAGHEAD

alert
airlifted
rainwater
theft
t a k e n
adrift
feathered, tendriled

inearthed

inearthing

few

fewer

FILL'D

White

eternal

dwindling

nattering
nightlife
Filled
withdrawn
(addled)

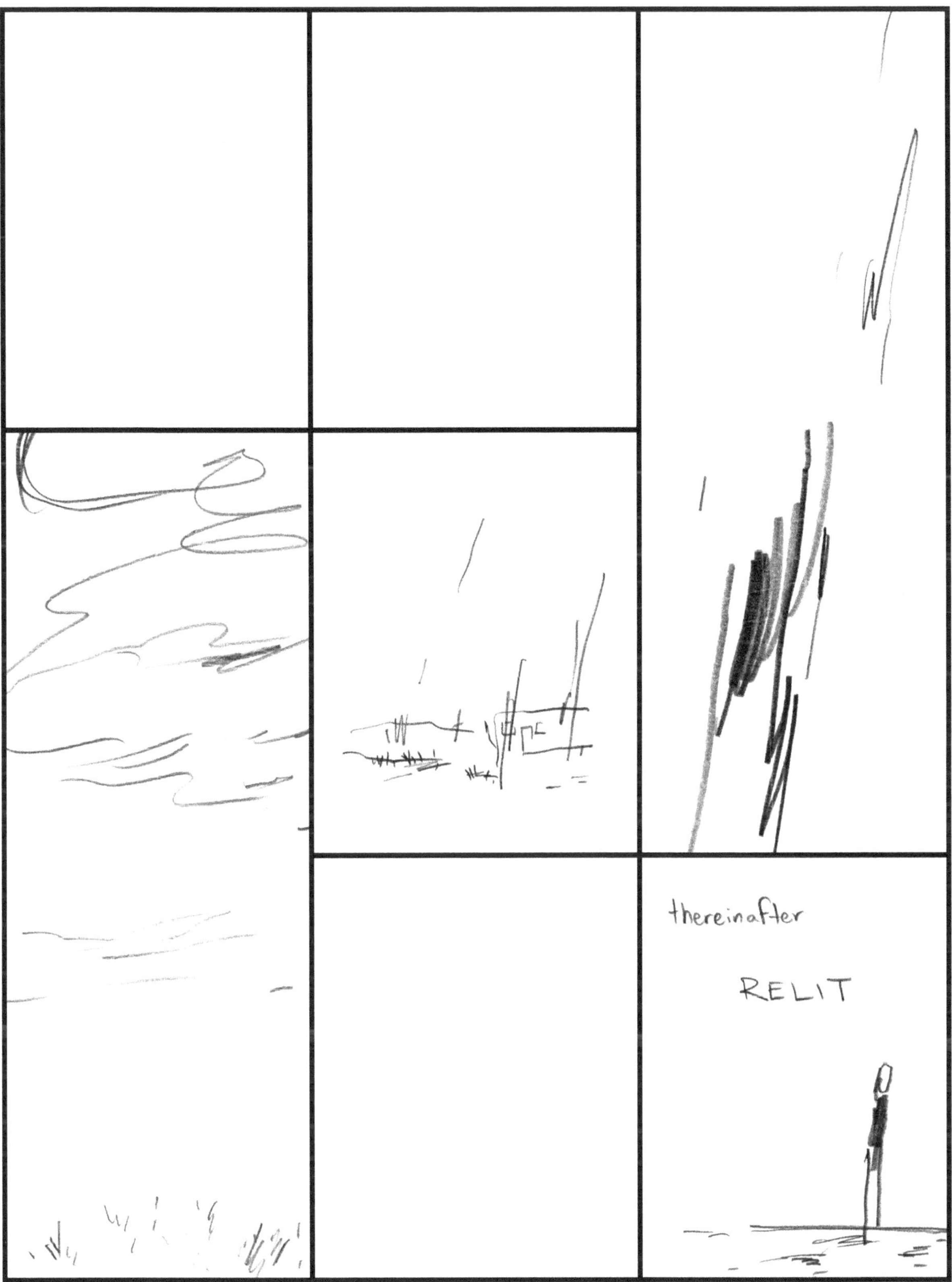

thereinafter

RELIT

KIND
thawed
threat
(indefinite)

airlifted?
thin relief
thin relief.

my name is
martin shears

unbelievable, martin.
i'm really at a loss here
you need to fix this.
now.
i know
i will

hi, my name is martin shears. i phoned a few minutes ago?

oh, well i don't actually have an appointment

it's a personal matter. well, no, it's a business matter, but—

yes. of course. no, i understand that.

please?

i promise it's really important

hi, yes i'm calling with regards to—

yes, i was told to call this number, and—

my name is martin shears, and i'm—

no, i can hold

yes, this is robert snively, and i'm a lawyer representing mr. martin shears . . .

those bags under your eyes are looking a little heavier, martin

if you're not careful

you're going to start looking middle aged

those bags under your eyes are looking to start looking middle aged

mr. snively, i think we could sort this out much more easily
if you could just
drop by
in person
mr. snively, i think we could sort this out much more easily
if you could just

SPLASH

nice haircut, shears

oh fuck off it's not that bad

hey, i'm being serious. it looks alright, man.

hell of an improvement over the mop top.

i've lived here my whole life. my family has been here for generations.

well i'm a lawyer, but i'm thinking about changing careers.

and i don't even remember where the scar came from!

no, i decided to go back to school. i'll be finished at the end of the year.

i moved here a few months ago — just started a new job

no, really, i'm pretty sure we've met before

i'd love to meet her!
you should bring her
by sometime.

maybe

i don't think i can
do that.

that would be great.

that's really not a good
idea.

no.

so tell me
about yourself

ha, no, i don't want to
hear what you DO...

tell me about YOU

what do you think?
it's . . .

oh, wait, i think we accidentally switched coats.

sorry!

wait, what are all these business cards for?

robert snively?

who's that?

would you really do that?
... did you?
of course i wouldn't
but
robert snively would

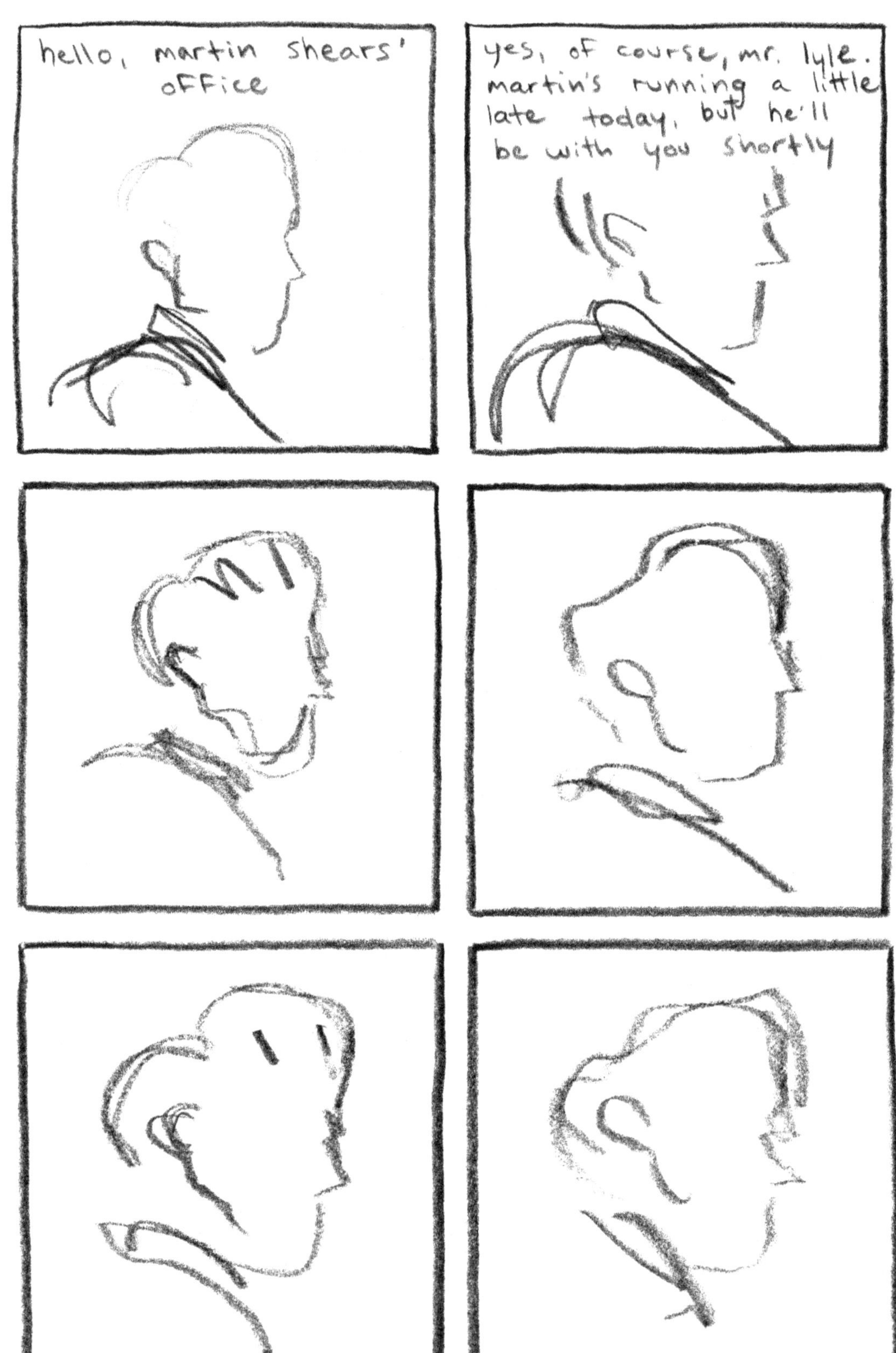

hello, martin shears' oFFice

yes, of course, mr. lyle. martin's running a little late today, but he'll be with you shortly

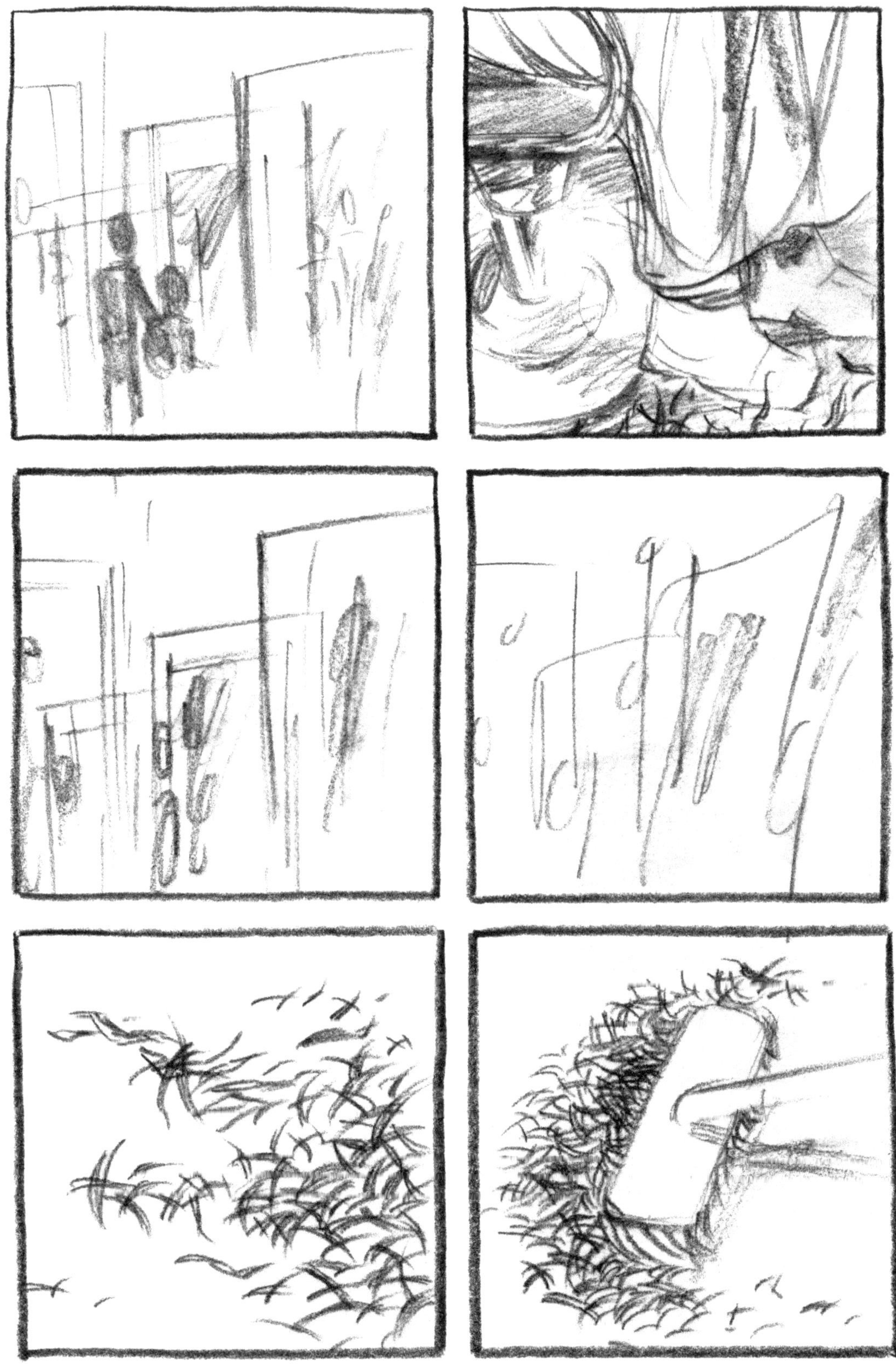

excuse me
excuse me

i've been looking everywhere for —

oh, i'm so sorry

i thought you were someone else

MARTIN   SHEARS
MARTIN   SHEARS
MARTIN   SHEARS
MARTIN   SHEARS
MARTIN   SHALES
MARTIN   SMIRLEY
MARTIN   SMARES
MARTIN   SPIRFLY
MARTIN   SPIRES
MARTIN   SEEVES
MARTIN   SILVER
MARTIN   SURLES
MARTIN   SURLEY
MARTIN   SLOPES
MARTIN   SPADE
MARTIN   SPARET
MARTIN   SPAD.
MARTIN
MARTIN
MARTIN

CAVITIES

I DON'T KNOW ALL THE DETAILS,
AND IT'S BEEN SO LONG.
TRY TO BE PATIENT WITH ME.

BECAUSE I WAS THERE AND I
UNDERSTOOD THEN AND I'M PRETTY
SURE I STILL UNDERSTAND NOW.
SO LISTEN,
AND I'LL
TELL YOU.

THE DENTIST LIKES HER JOB.
SHE HAS ONE ASSISTANT. HER
EX-HUSBAND, PETER, IS ONE OF HER
PATIENTS AND HE REFUSES TO GO TO ANYONE
ELSE BECAUSE HE SAYS THAT SHE'S THE BEST.

THE DENTIST KNOWS THE WAY HE MEANS
IT BUT THAT'S NOT THE WAY SHE TAKES IT.

WHEN HER
EX-HUSBAND COMES
IN FOR CHECK-UPS,
THEY DON'T TALK
VERY MUCH.

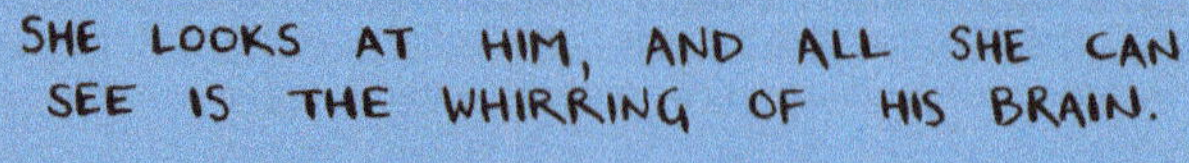

SHE LOOKS AT HIM, AND ALL SHE CAN
SEE IS THE WHIRRING OF HIS BRAIN.

IT SEEMS EXHAUSTING.

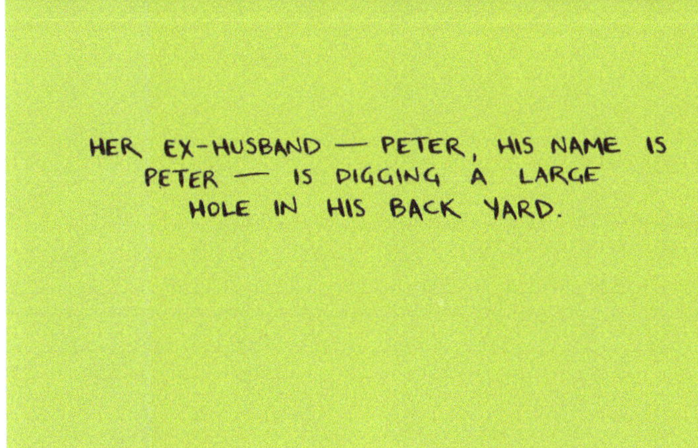
HER EX-HUSBAND — PETER, HIS NAME IS PETER — IS DIGGING A LARGE HOLE IN HIS BACK YARD.

MARSHALL — A FRIEND OF PETER'S, ANOTHER PATIENT — TOLD HER ABOUT THE HOLE.

SOMETIMES HER ASSISTANT MAKES LITTLE JOKES ABOUT THE HOLE, AND THE DENTIST LAUGHS EVEN THOUGH THE JOKES AREN'T FUNNY.

PETER HAS BEEN TALKING ABOUT THE HOLE FOR A LONG TIME, SO IT'S GREAT THAT HE'S FINALLY DOING IT.

AT THE END OF A LONG DAY, THE DENTIST WILL SOMETIMES STAND ALONE OUTSIDE HER OFFICE AND WATCH COLORED SHADOWS GLIDE ACROSS THE WALL.

SHE CHEWS HER FINGERS METHODICALLY, UNTIL THEY START TO BLEED.
THE WALL OUTSIDE HER OFFICE IS A PALE GREEN AND SHE WOULD LIKE IT TO BE A QUIET ORANGE.

MAYBE HER EYES ARE GETTING WORSE.

SHE DOES USE THEM ALL DAY — AND SHE WAS SO SICKLY AS A CHILD.

SHE NEEDS TO ASK PETER WHEN HE'LL BE DONE DIGGING.

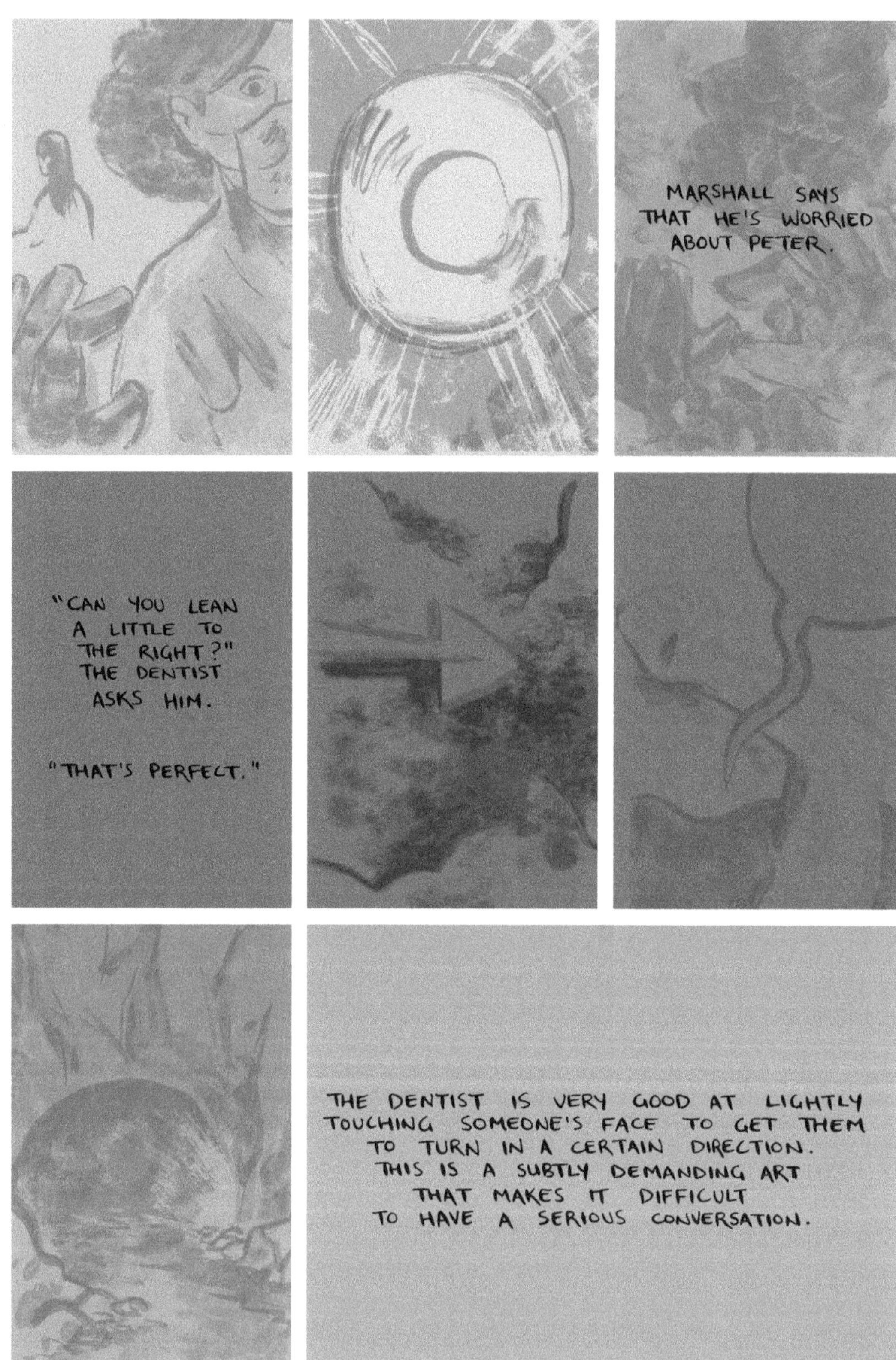

MARSHALL SAYS THAT HE'S WORRIED ABOUT PETER.
"CAN YOU LEAN A LITTLE TO THE RIGHT?" THE DENTIST ASKS HIM.
"THAT'S PERFECT."
THE DENTIST IS VERY GOOD AT LIGHTLY TOUCHING SOMEONE'S FACE TO GET THEM TO TURN IN A CERTAIN DIRECTION. THIS IS A SUBTLY DEMANDING ART THAT MAKES IT DIFFICULT TO HAVE A SERIOUS CONVERSATION.

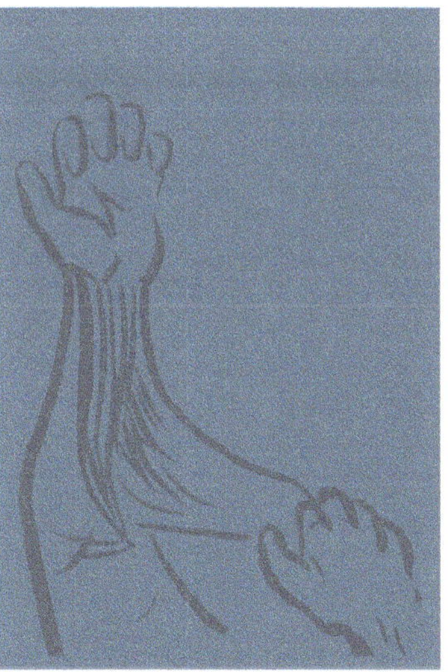

MARSHALL IS WORRIED ABOUT PETER, BUT NOT
BECAUSE HE'S DIGGING THE HOLE. PETER HAS
BEEN TALKING ABOUT THE HOLE FOR
A LONG TIME, SO IT'S GREAT THAT
HE'S FINALLY DOING IT.

MARSHALL IS WORRIED BECAUSE PETER HAS BEEN
GOING DOWN INTO THE HOLE FOR HOURS,
ALL BY HIMSELF. NORMALLY, PETER DOESN'T
LIKE TO BE ALONE. HE SAYS IT'S
HARDER FOR HIM TO THINK.

THAT NIGHT, THE DENTIST AND HER ASSISTANT GO TO SEE THE HOLE.
THEY DON'T TALK — THEY JUST LOOK AT IT.

THE DENTIST GOES TO SEE PETER AND THEY HAVE A CONVERSATION.

THE DENTIST REMEMBERS PARTS OF IT.

SHE REMEMBERS
FEELING UNEASY.

SHE COULD TELL
THAT HER
EX-HUSBAND WAS
TALKING FASTER
THAN HE WAS
THINKING.

THE NEXT WEEK, WHEN THE DENTIST AND
HER ASSISTANT GO BACK TO THE HOLE,
IT'S DIFFERENT. THE WALLS ARE BRICK AND
THERE'S A LADDER AND IT GOES VERY FAR DOWN.

IT FEELS WRONG TO BE THERE.

THEY CLIMB DOWN THE LADDER AND WALK DOWN
A DARK HALLWAY. THEY HOLD HANDS.
THEY DON'T TALK ABOUT THE PRESENCE
THAT THEY FEEL SWIRLING BEHIND THEM.

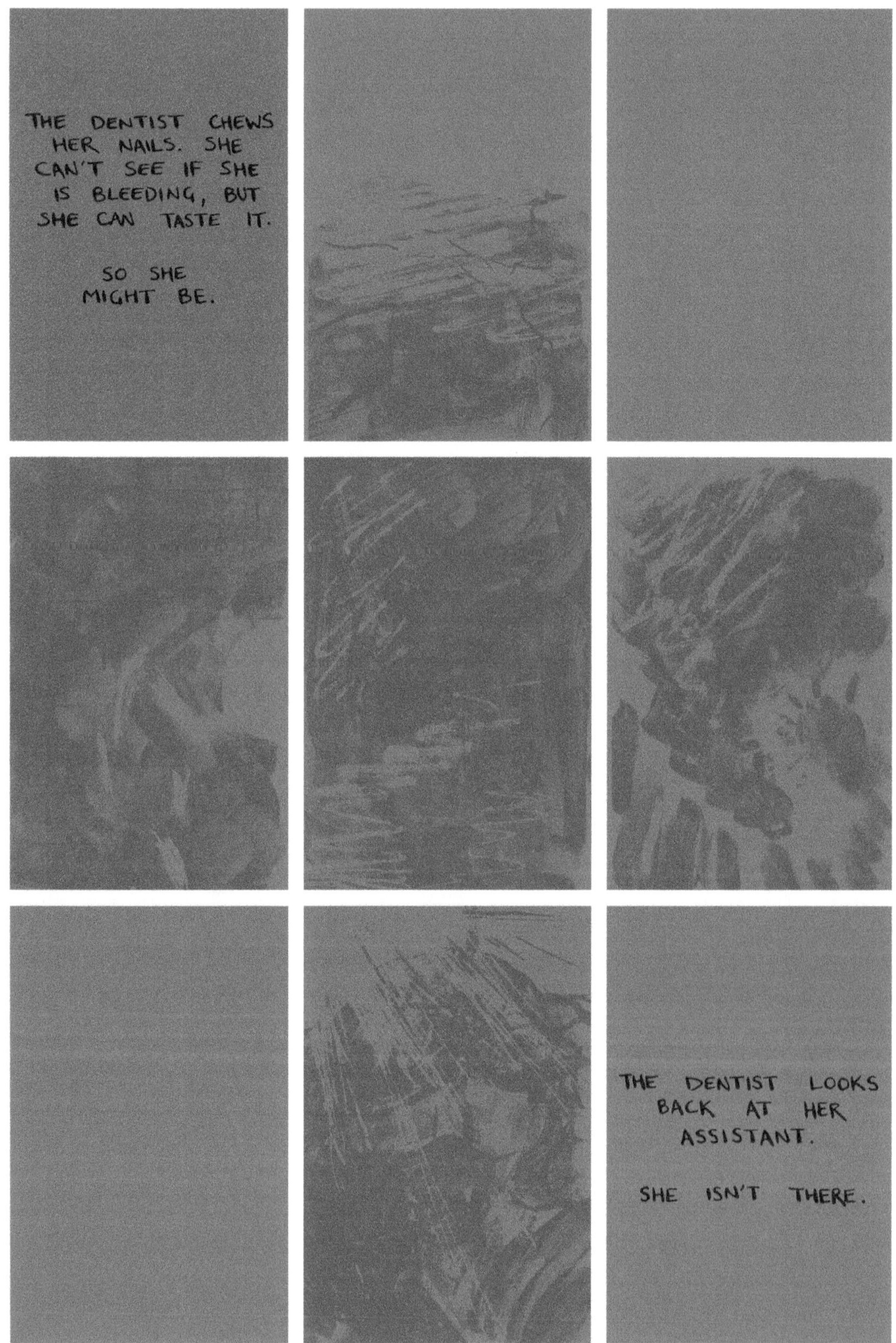

THE DENTIST CHEWS HER NAILS. SHE CAN'T SEE IF SHE IS BLEEDING, BUT SHE CAN TASTE IT.

SO SHE MIGHT BE.
THE DENTIST LOOKS BACK AT HER ASSISTANT.

SHE ISN'T THERE.

AFTER SHE CLIMBS
OUT OF THE HOLE,
SHE DOESN'T TALK
TO PETER AGAIN
FOR MANY YEARS.

IT'S BETTER
THAT WAY.

dark   light

based on words by
warren craghead

lines on window
dark out light in

a jar in the
middle gets lost

a pie. once i ate
grass, it was not
good, but imagine

a moon up
light leaves
from below

lines on window
dark out light in

window
light

r a t

s

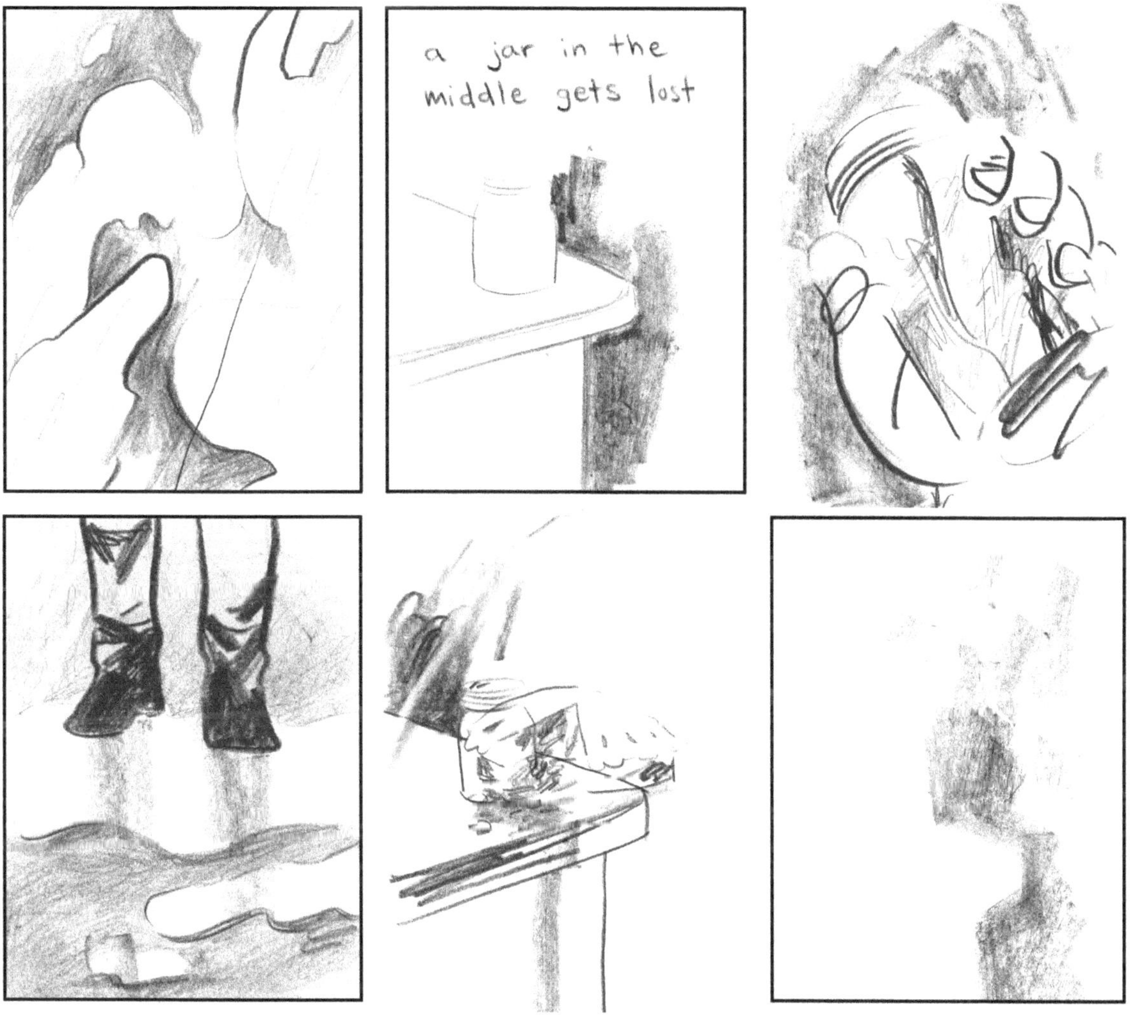

a jar in the
middle gets lost

iddle
s
a pie. once i ate
grass, it was not
good, but imagine
imagine

s was t
e
d

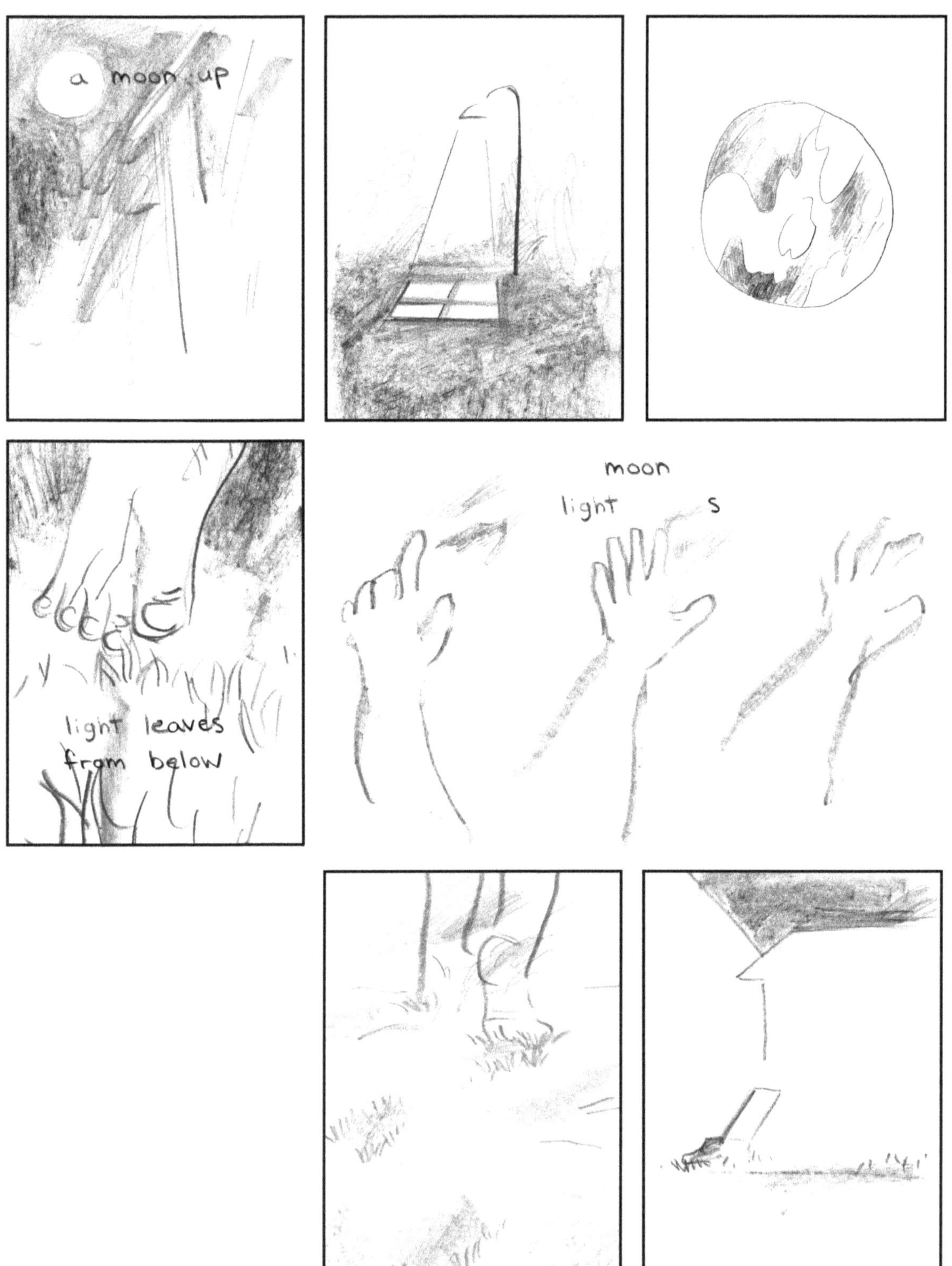

a moon up
light leaves
from below
moon
light
s

a pie. once i ate
grass, it was not
good, but imagine

imagine

AFTER THE FIRE

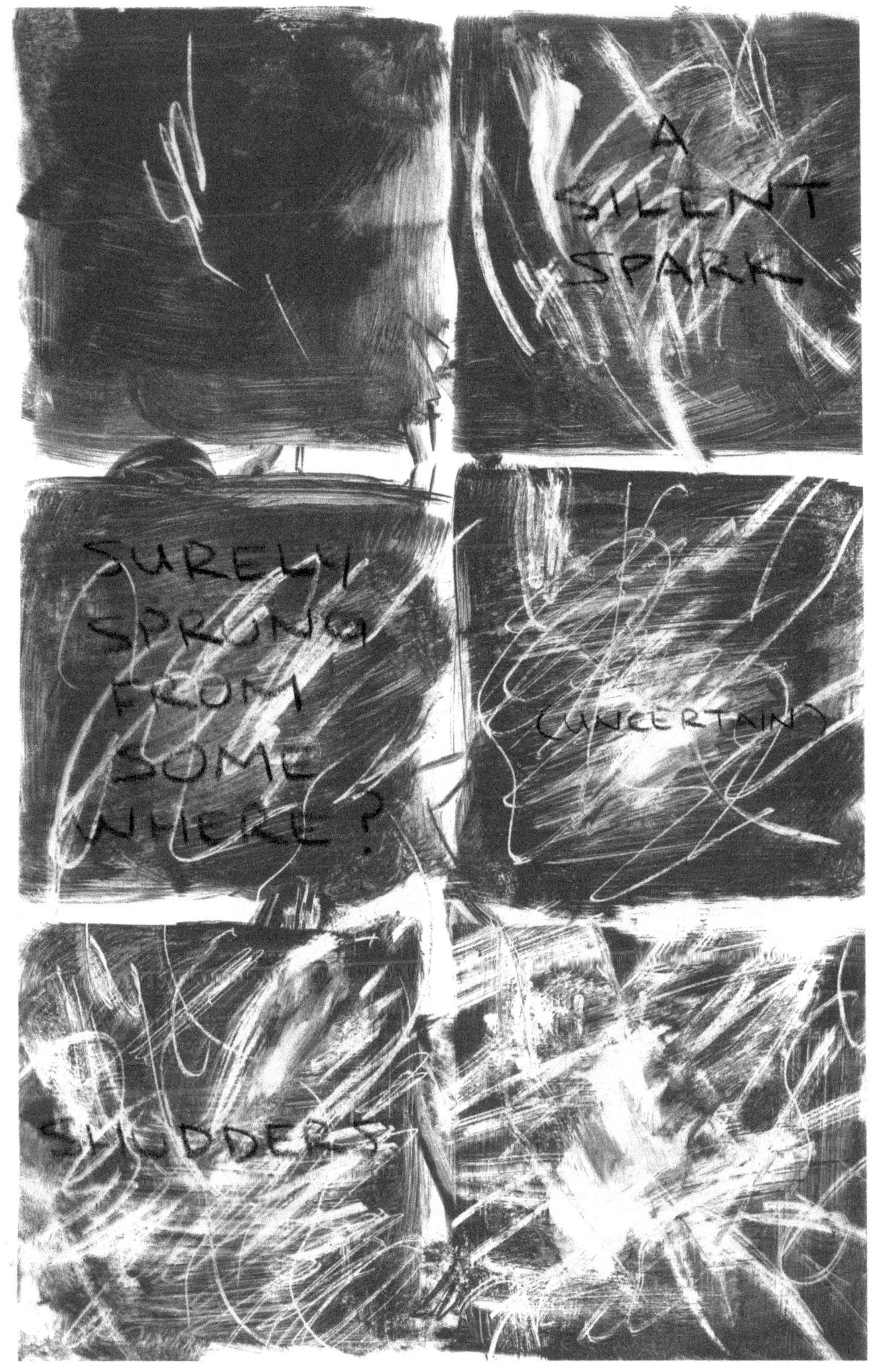
A SILENT SPARK
SURELY SPRUNG FROM SOMEWHERE?
(UNCERTAIN)
SHUDDERS

SCATTERS

BURNED
EX
ITS
EMBERS
SHUDDER

LUNG
THROAT
TIGHT
HOT

SILK
RIVERS
OF
FLAME

THEY
BRING US
NOTHING

SUCH
NOTHING

AFTER THE FIRE
WE BURST
INTO FLAMES.

AFTER THE FIRE
THE SMOKE
STARTED
CLEARING

AFTER THE FIRE
WE WERE DOUSED
IN SILENCE.

AFTER THE FIRE
THE EMBERS
REMEMBERED.

AFTER THE FIRE
OUR VOICES GREW
SOFTER.

AFTER THE FIRE
THERE ARE THINGS
THAT WERE BURNED.

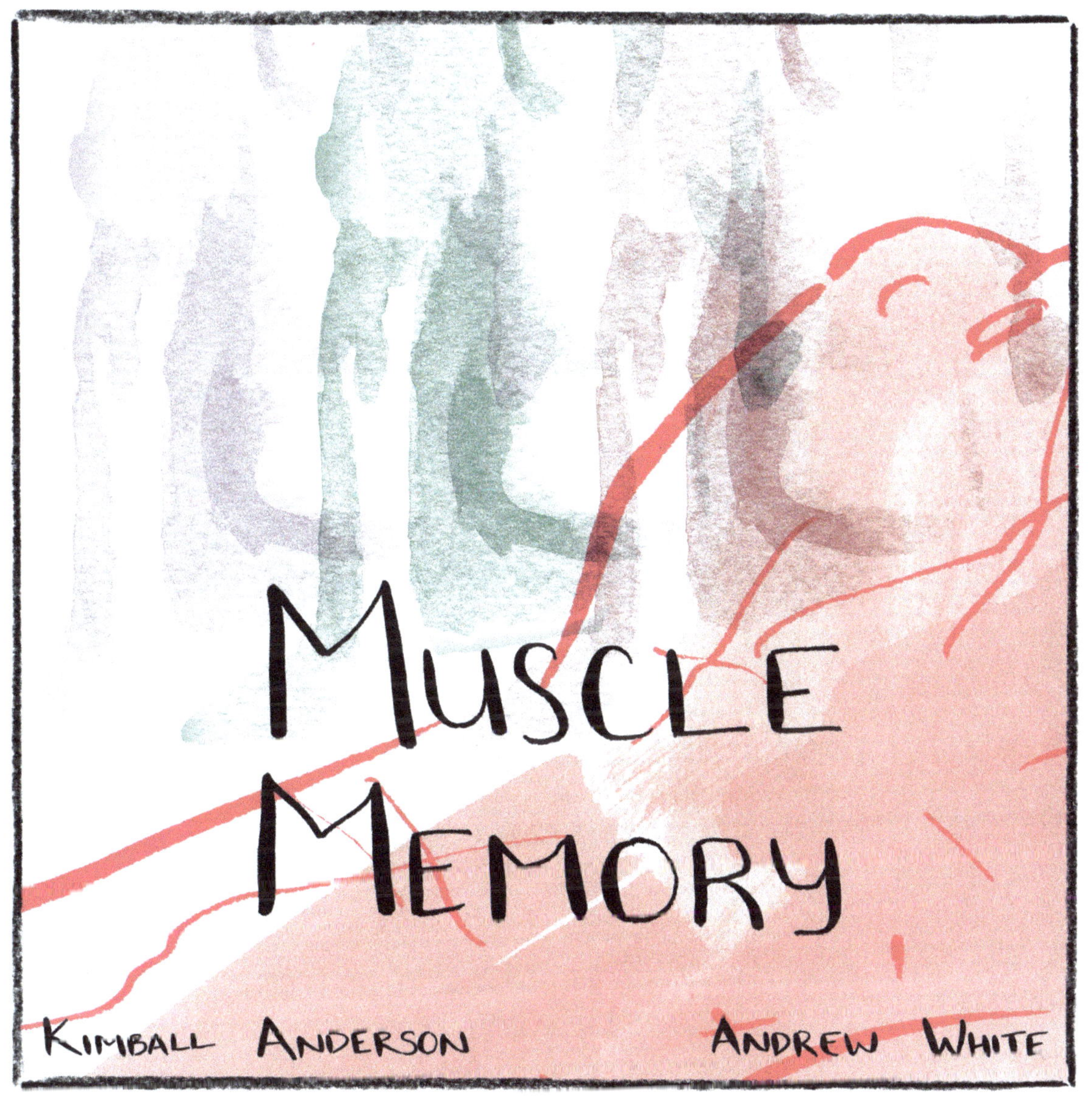
MUSCLE
MEMORY
KIMBALL ANDERSON
ANDREW WHITE

THERE IS FLOUR STUCK TO THE INSIDE
OF A MEASURING CUP. THE ONLY UNCHANGED
SPECKS, AS THE FLOUR BECOMES BISCUIT OR
COOKIE OR BREAD.

THE EGG WHITE GOES FROM CLEAR TO OPAQUE IN THE
PAN. IT ALREADY CONTAINED ITS CHANGE, IT ALREADY
HAD THE CAPACITY FOR ITS TRANSFORMATION.

I WOKE THIS MORNING THE SAME AS I GO TO
BED TONIGHT. BUT DURING THE DAY, DURING THE
DAY I AM BECOMING.

ME-WHO-WAS-ONCE. ME-WHO-WILL-BE. I'VE BEEN
THINKING ABOUT IT TODAY.

EXPECTATIONS, I GUESS.

PREPARED
WITH SLOW DELIBERATION
UNDETERRED CONSTERNATION
YES

FORMS FILLED
FILLED FORMS
FEEL OUT OF PLACE
FUMBLING TOWARDS A WAY FORWARD
FORMS FILLED
FILLED FORMS
FEEL OUT OF PLACE
FUMBLING TOWARDS A WAY FORWARD

PREPARED
AS ANTICIPATION CLOSES IN
PRECIPITATION OF PLODDING PIECES
AS IF READINESS REQUIRES REPETITION
REPLICATION REVERBERATES ?
REVEALING

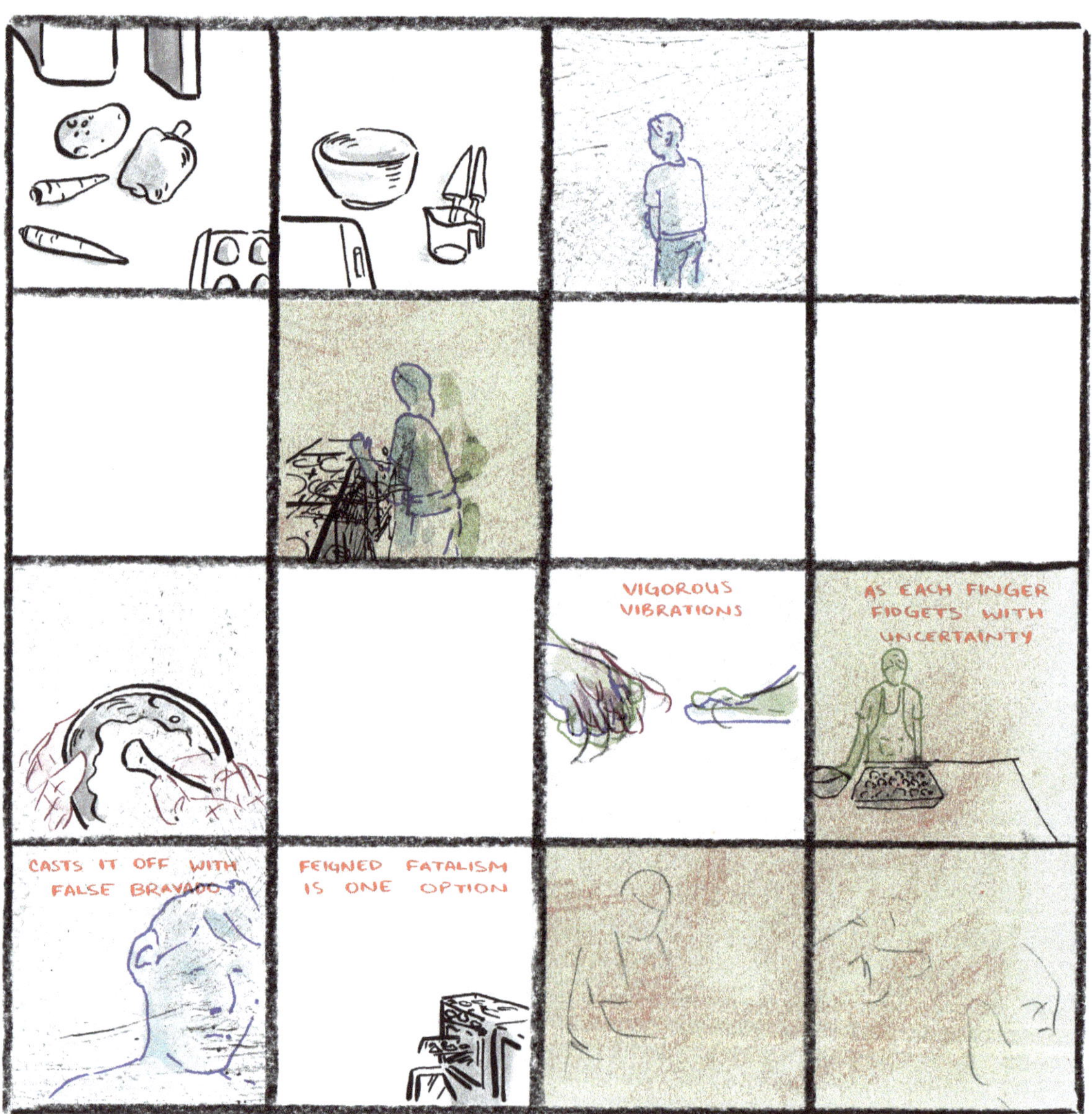

VIGOROUS VIBRATIONS
AS EACH FINGER FIDGETS WITH UNCERTAINTY
CASTS IT OFF WITH FALSE BRAVADO
FEIGNED FATALISM IS ONE OPTION

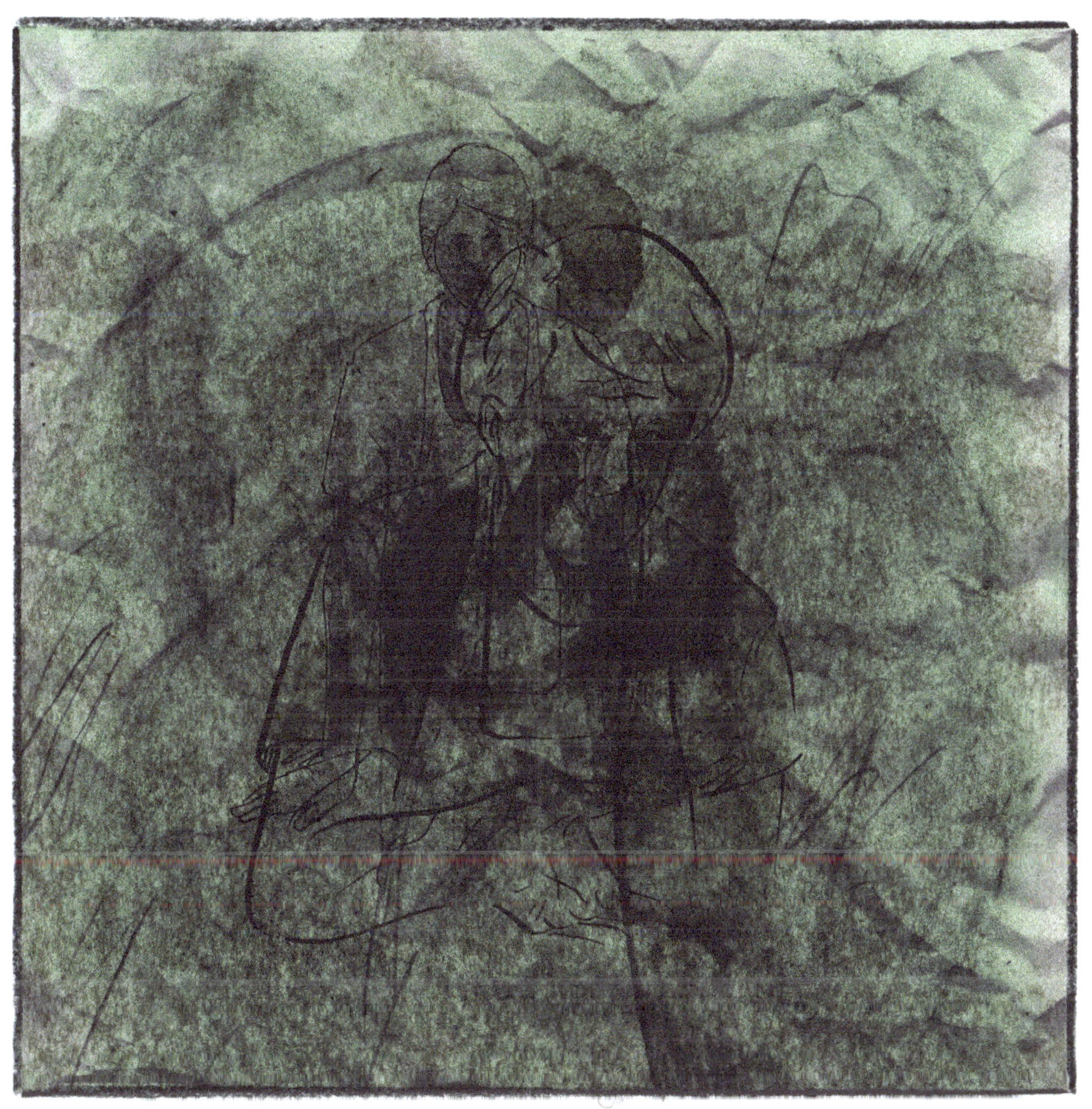

TINY MOMENTS WILL ASSUREDLY ACCUMULATE
TINGES OF VERTIGO WILL UNDOUBTEDLY ASSIMILATE

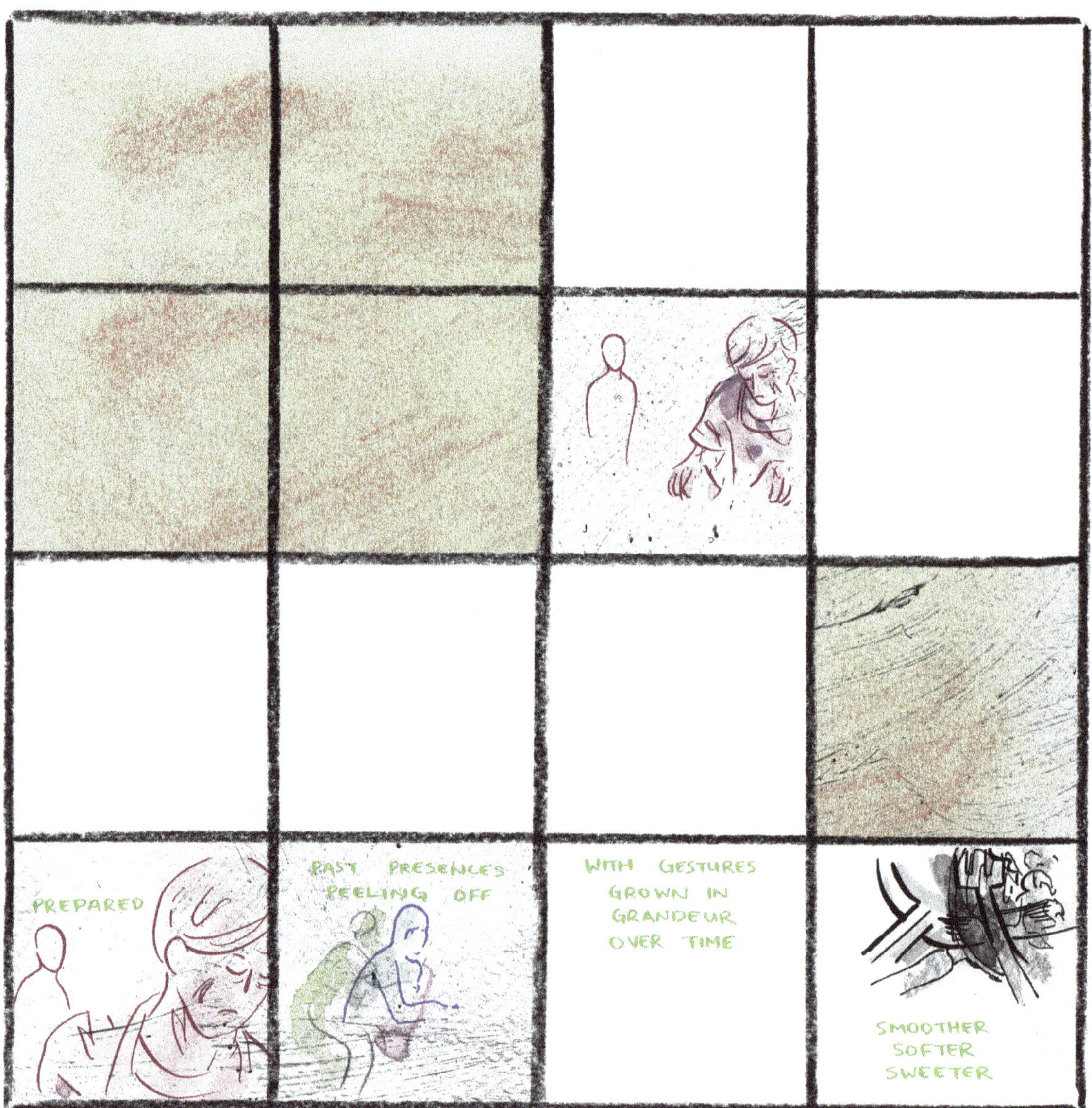

PREPARED
PAST PRESENCES
PEELING OFF
WITH GESTURES
GROWN IN
GRANDEUR
OVER TIME
SMOOTHER
SOFTER
SWEETER

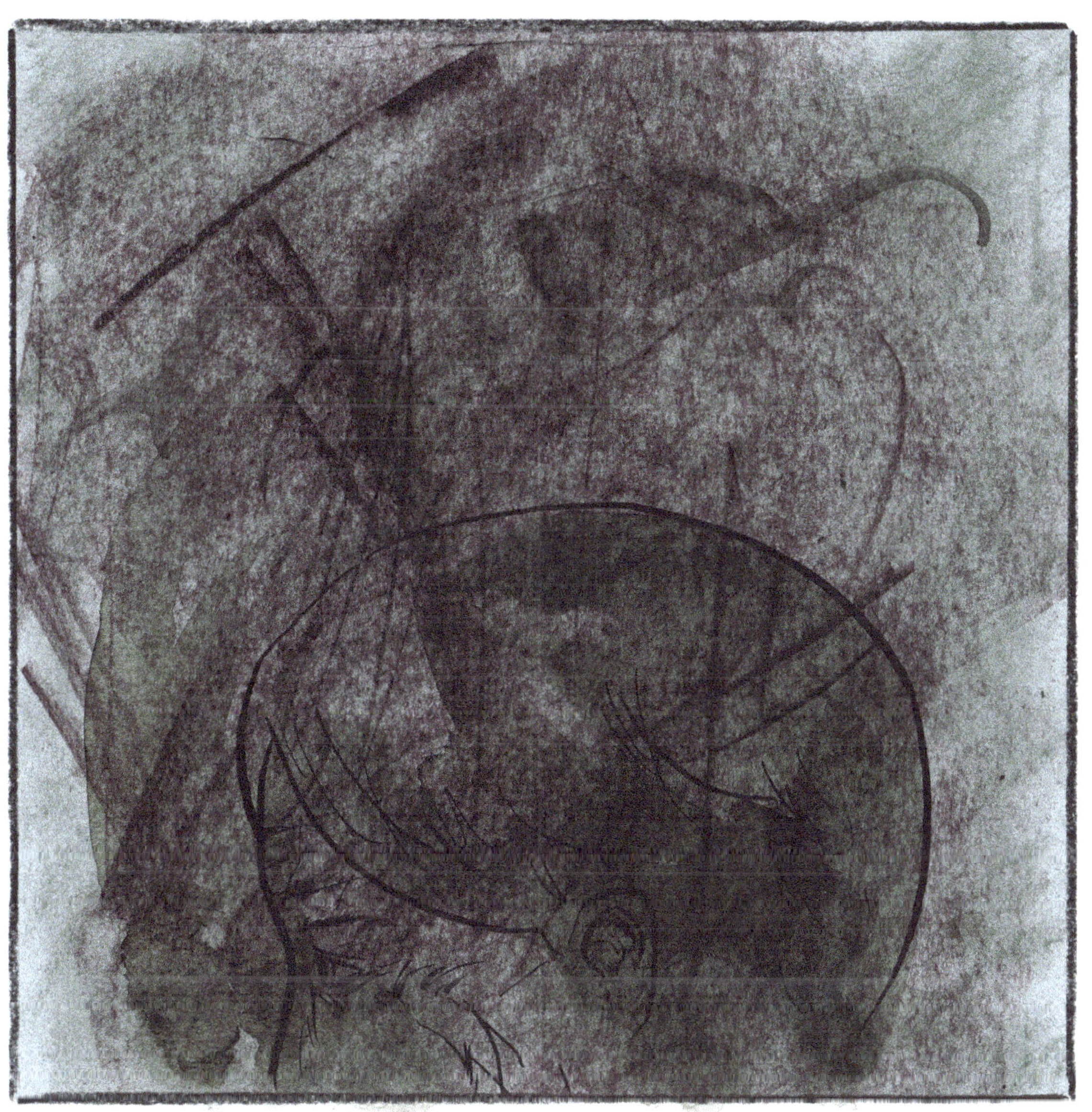

FEEL OUT OF PLACE
FUMBLING TOWARDS A WAY FORWARD
AS EACH FINGER FIDGETS WITH UNCERTAINTY
TINY MOMENTS WILL ASSUREDLY ACCUMULATE

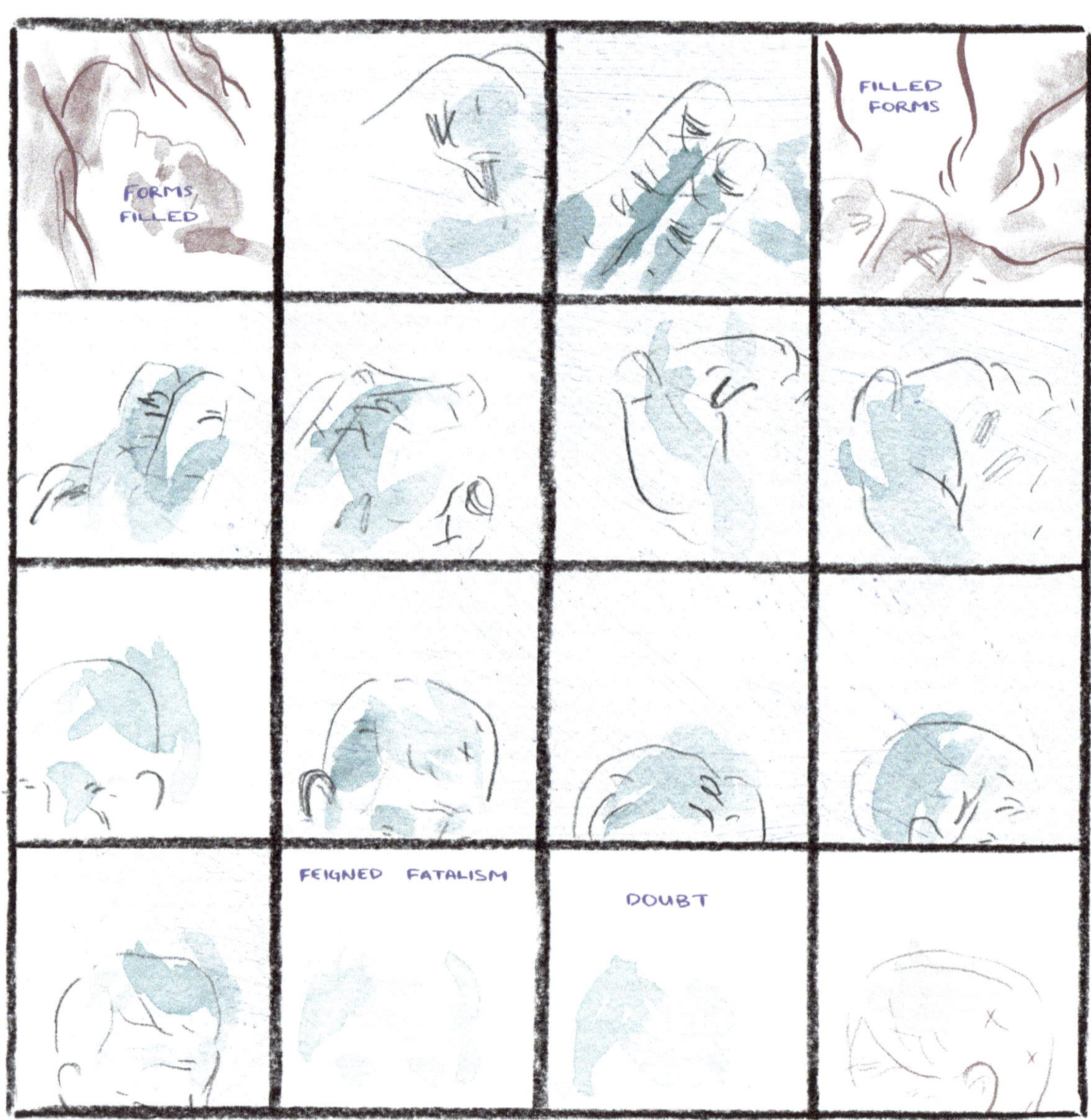

FORMS
FILLED
FILLED
FORMS
FEIGNED FATALISM
DOUBT

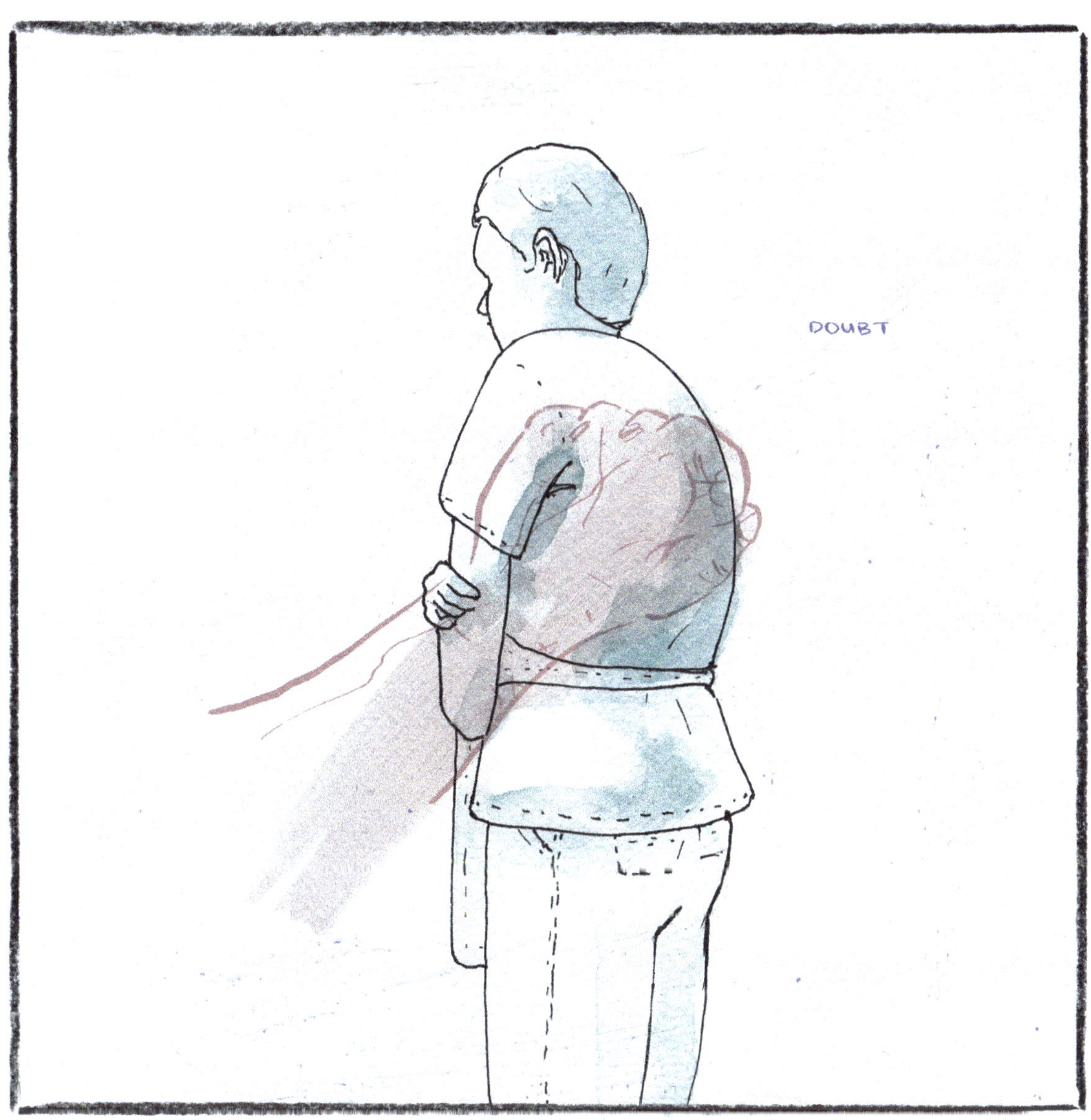
DOUBT

PREPARED
WITH SLOW
DELIBERATION
FUMBLING TOWARDS
A WAY FORWARD
PREPARED
VIGOROUS
VIBRATIONS
PREPARED

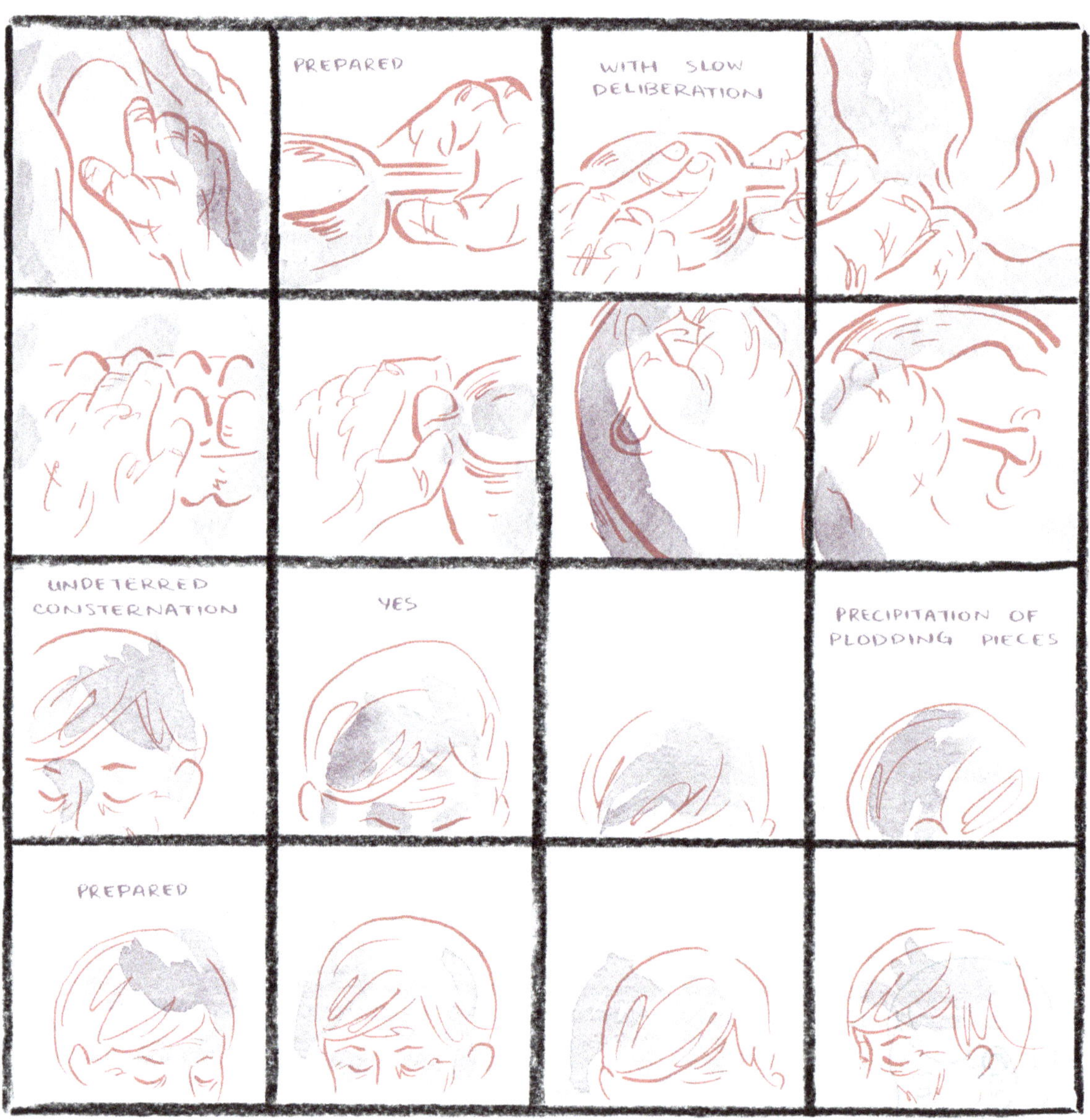

PREPARED
WITH SLOW DELIBERATION
UNDETERRED CONSTERNATION
YES
PRECIPITATION OF PLODDING PIECES
PREPARED

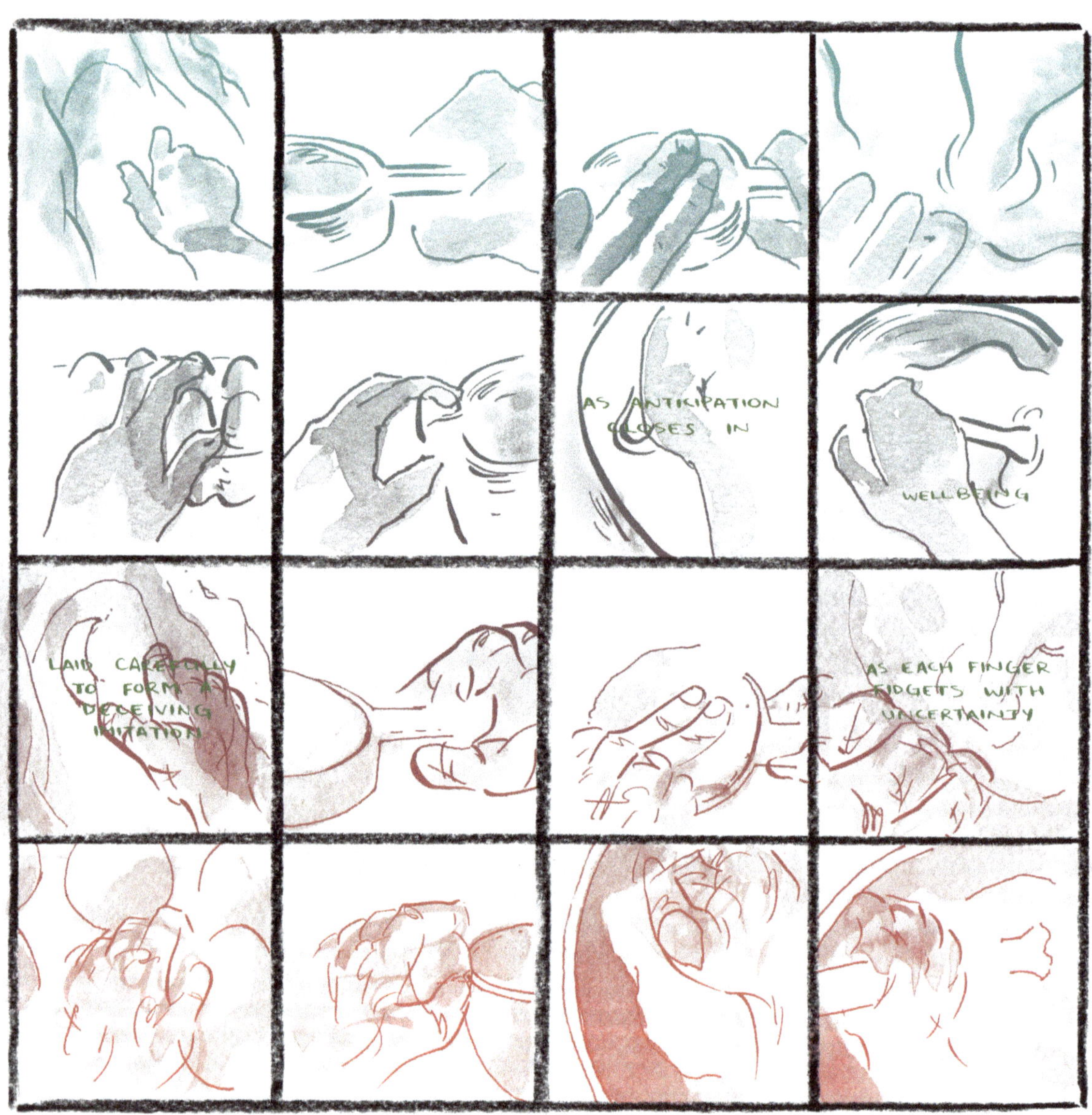

AS ANTICIPATION CLOSES IN
WELLBEING
LAID CAREFULLY TO FORM A DECEIVING IMITATION
AS EACH FINGER FIDGETS WITH UNCERTAINTY

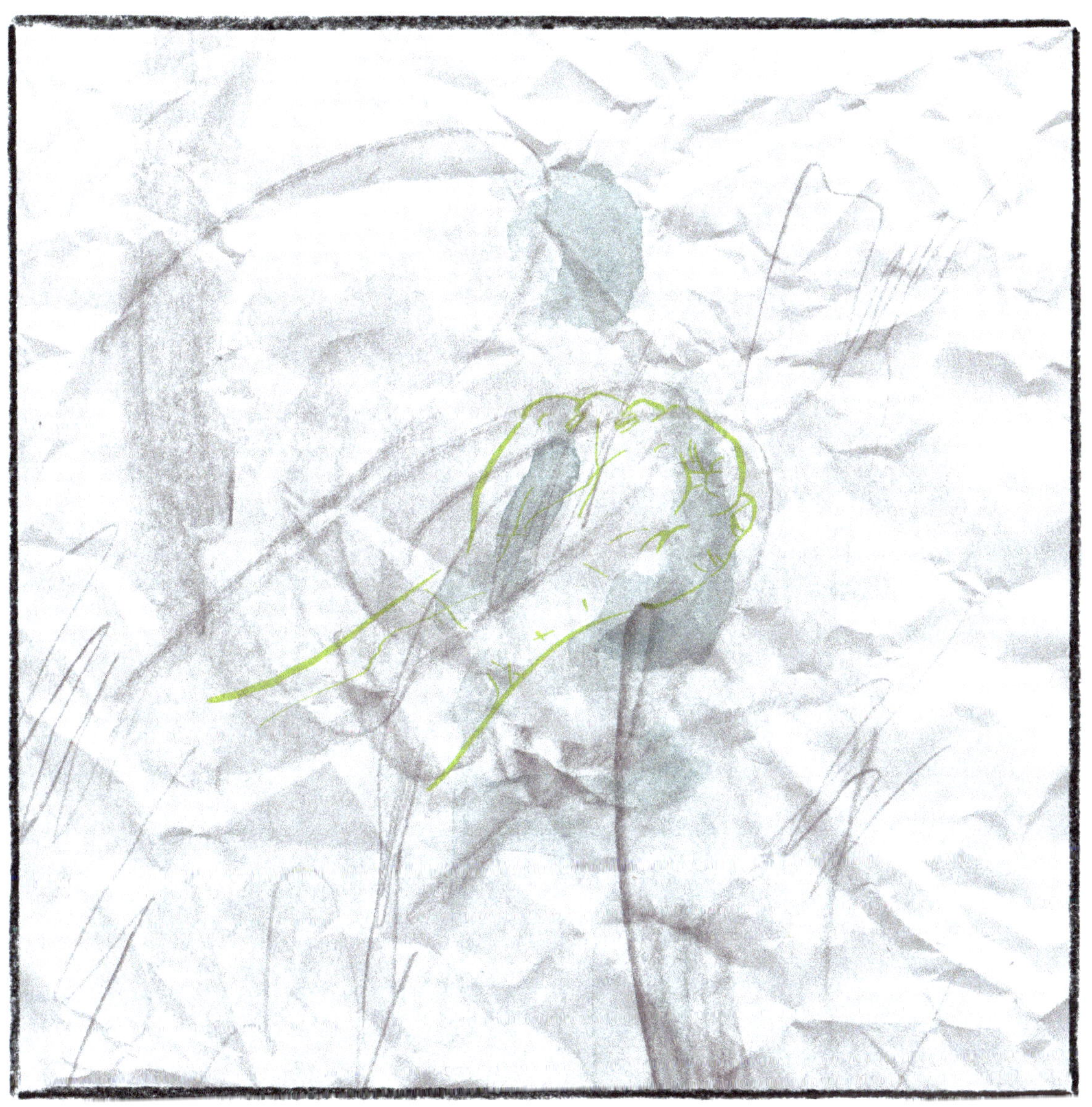

PREPARED
FIND A
THOROUGHFARE
OR BE
INVIGORATING
REVERBERATES
REVEALING
TINY
MOMENTS
SMOOTHER
SOFTER
SWEETER

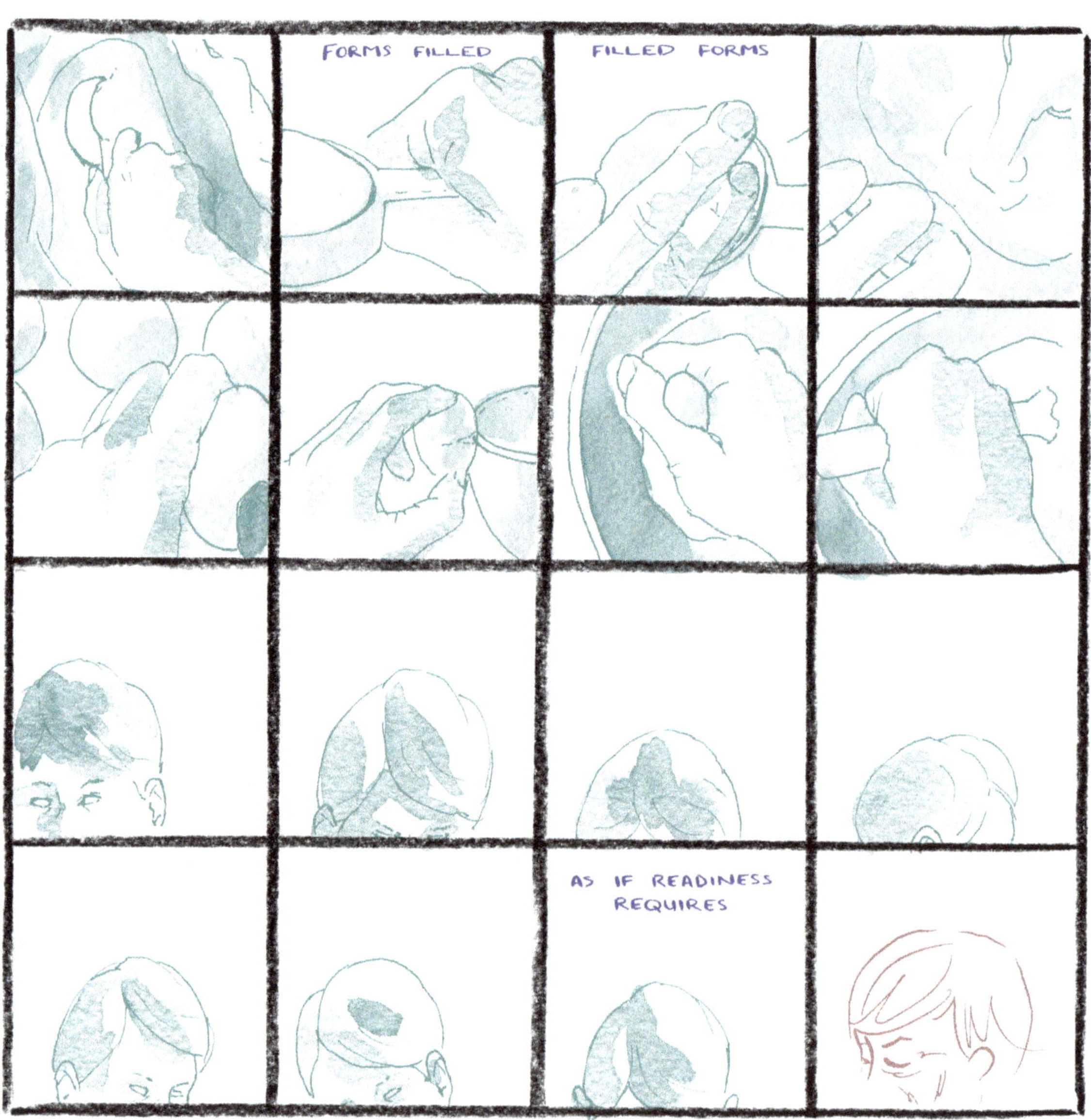
FORMS FILLED
FILLED FORMS
AS IF READINESS
REQUIRES

REPETITION

I ONLY WATCHED HER AT FIRST. I MAY HAVE EVEN CONVINCED MYSELF THAT WATCHING COULD BE ENOUGH. BUT ALMOST BEFORE I KNEW IT, SHE WAS GUIDING MY HANDS INTO PLACE AND SHOWING MY EYES HOW TO SEE.

IT WASN'T A QUESTION OF REPETITION, SHE TAUGHT ME, BUT OF TINY CHANGES. INFINITE VARIATIONS. YOU HAD TO ADAPT TO THE SUBTLETIES OF THE INGREDIENTS, OF THE OVEN, OF THE AIR.

IT WAS INCREDIBLY SELFLESS, THE WAY SHE LET HERSELF FADE QUIETLY INTO THE BACKGROUND. I THOUGHT I WAS IN CONTROL LONG BEFORE SHE TRULY LET GO OF THE REINS.

RIPPLES

WHEN DEBBIE WENT OUTSIDE,
SHE VIBRATED. HER BODY BEGGED
FOR NEW TEXTURES.

BUT PINK HUES WARNED THAT
NIGHT WAS CREEPING
TOWARDS HER,

SO SHE WENT BACK INSIDE
THE HOUSE AND CLOSED
THE DOOR.

DEBBIE HADN'T ALWAYS WAITED. THERE WAS A TIME WHEN SHE EXTENDED HER HANDS OUT TOWARDS THE WORLD, HER JOINTS HUMMING AS SHE GRASPED AT THE SWEET HUES OF EVERYTHING.

MISTY SOUNDS PASSED BY HER OUTSTRETCHED FINGERS AND BILLOWED AROUND HER.

HER FEET BURROWED INTO THE DIRT AND HER TOES CURLED.

BUT YEARS ALWAYS ACCUMULATE. SO DEBBIE WAS WAITING NOW.

HER HOUSE WAS NOT SMALL, AND MANY OF ITS ROOMS WERE EMPTY MORE OFTEN THAN NOT.

THOUGH THIS DIDN'T BOTHER DEBBIE.

"I HAVE LIVED A THOUSAND YEARS," SHE SAID. (THIS WAS A LIE.)

"AND I HAVE SEEN MANY THINGS."

(THAT PART WAS TRUE.)

"HELLO," DEBBIE SAID.
 DIDN'T ANSWER.

THEY LOOKED AT EACH OTHER.
THE AIR BETWEEN THEM CREAKED.

"I'M HAPPY YOU'RE HERE,"
DEBBIE TOLD ⌇, CHOOSING HER
WORDS WITH WAVERING PRECISION.

"BUT I'VE ENJOYED THE WAITING,
AND I'M SORRY TO SEE IT END."

⌇ NODDED IN UNDERSTANDING.

THEIR HANDS CLASPED THEN,
OR COLLAPSED, OR DIDN'T.

THEY REACHED THROUGH EACH
OTHER UNTIL SOMETHING SHATTERED.

WIND

MOVING THROUGH DAYS LIKE
THERE'S SOMETHING TO BE REACHED
TO BE FOUND

THIS YEAR
MY PLANS
SIT UNATTENDED
TEETERING
CON
FINED
CONFLICTED

DESPITE OUR
DEEPEST HOPES
AND MOST
SINCERE PLEAS

TIME REFUSES
TO SLOW
DOWN.

the old capital
CRUMBLES
faint
scent
of old
books burning

MARCH (2012)

This story is inspired by an Italo Calvino story and contains the first appearance of several topics that continue to preoccupy me: adapting or combining text, repetition, and memory. Calvino is still one of my favorite writers, and the way he builds short stories into broader, interconnected narratives was a big inspiration for me around this time (see also Alice Munro and Elizabeth Strout, though I hadn't yet discovered either of them in 2012).

BLACK PILLARS (2014-2015)

This is the opening sequence to Black Pillars, a two issue series that I drew in 2014 and 2015. I wasn't happy enough with the full issues to include them in this collection, but I like both this piece itself and the fact that it marks the first appearance of another favorite theme: an ongoing preoccupation with breathing as a way of communicating rhythm, and with formal approaches to depicting the experience of breathing. Perhaps the single biggest influence on my ideas about this are an untitled one page strip in Cusp, by Tom Herpich. If you've read it, you probably know the one I mean.

PAWN (2014)

Had I started to see risographed comics when I drew this? Maybe. I know that a bigger inspiration for the layering here was Jordan Crane's silkscreen work. This was drawn very shortly after We Will Remain, a one-person anthology published by Retrofit Comics that I decided not to include here because I'm not particularly happy with most of those stories. Plus, that's still the comic of mine with the biggest print run, so people who want it probably already have it!

WHILE A SOFT FOG WANDERS (2014)

Condensed and lightly resequenced for this collection, because the original version now reads to me like it was saying the same thing over and over again but less articulately each time. Hopefully this version communicates the same ideas with more elegance. I still like the drawings and the mood they create.

TWO UNTITLED COLLABORATIONS (2014, with Derik Badman)

Derik Badman is an excellent cartoonist, even if he isn't making comics as often these days, and a big influence in me through both his work and his wide-ranging tastes in comics and literature. The first story, in full color, was produced by passing Photoshop files back and forth with perhaps a few other tricks/constraints that I can no longer recall. The second story, which is still one of my favorite comics I have drawn, uses code Derik had written at the time to randomly alter and sequence photos (in this case, photos I had taken) to create comics. I then redrew some of those automatic comics in pen and ink.

FILL'D (2014, with Warren Craghead)

A split mini that Warren and I drew in the few weeks before the Small Press Expo (SPX). Warren's comic in this one was called Empty'd and was based on words that I sent him. Throughout the period covered in this collection, SPX was the only comics show at which I exhibited each year, and for several of those years I shared a table with Warren. It was incredibly encouraging—and still is!—to get to know someone who had produced amazing, singular work for as long and with as much consistency as Warren. His example helped me see how it might be possible to continue making comics for my whole life, even in the absence of any real financial rewards.

MY NAME IS MARTIN SHEARS (2014)

This was the first comic I drew on tracing paper, a surface I still value for its disposability and for the interesting ways it handles materials from pencils to markers. This comic was originally published in four separate versions, each containing a slightly different version of the story. I imagined that people would see images of the comic online, or read a review of it, and be confused because that telling didn't match their own version of the story, thereby underscoring the book's thematic focus on question of identity and perception. As far as I know, this never happened. For this collection, I selected the version I liked best.

CAVITIES (2015)

Both this and the following story, After the Fire, were drawn straight to ink on Dur-a-lar transparencies. The coloring here was heavily inspired by Josef Albers' Interactions of Color, which I had read for the first time in 2015 as I was beginning to think about how I wanted to approach color comics. Nominated for the the Slate Cartoonist Studio Prize in 2016. Relettered and lightly edited for this collection.

DARK LIGHT (2015, with Warren Craghead)

Of course, after I had made a comic based on Warren's drawing for Fill'd, I made a comic based on his words here. This was again a split mini produced for SPX and has been reformatted for this collection.

AFTER THE FIRE (2015)

This piece is the most heavily edited for this collection. The original version had a narrative component that, unfortunately, didn't come together and feels unsalvageable now. But I liked the drawings too much to cut the story completely.

MUSCLE MEMORY (2016, with Kimball Anderson)

This comic, a collaboration with Kimball Anderson, really feels like a miracle to me because it reads as a true, seamless collaboration but I can't recall except in the broadest sense how we achieved that effect. I remember that we agreed on a general thrust for the story and each produced a set of drawings. Then we passed Photoshop files back and forth that combined and sequenced those drawings. But it's easy to imagine how that process might have resulted in a comic that was disjointed if not completely unreadable. Kimball remains one of my closest friends in comics and their work is an ongoing inspiration.

RIPPLES (2016)

This was originally a series of large drawings—most of the individual panels were drawn at 11x14—that slowly condensed into a short narrative. It was first published in Ink Brick No. 8, where it benefitted substantially from edits by Alexander Rothman.

COMICS WORKBOOK STRIPS (2012-2015)

The one page, eight panel comics that appear at the beginning and the end of this book are excerpted from the hundreds of strips I drew for Comics Workbook, the online publication headed first by Frank Santoro and then by Juan Fernandez.

An Interview With Andrew White
Conducted by Alec Berry

Andrew's comics utilize abstraction, and they can focus on quiet things. But past the first glance, most all of them revolve around a story.

I mean, he has made comics that are more so poems or meditations or reflections, but his overall focus and progression is toward narrative. Andrew's comics (particularly those featured in We Are Breathing) show the reader a story from a hidden or unconsidered perspective. Maybe even one that's inanimate or spectral.

That element fosters abstract imagery and sometimes loose thematic connections, but it presents possibilities for stories. It asks the reader questions, like: What's sitting right in front of you, or out your window, or inside a memory? What's going on there with it? How can it be shown or viewed? What do you recognize, or want to say, or struggle with that's inherent to it?

While Andrew's work can challenge a reader, it can connect them to their experience of the world. It can drop them inside a particular vantage point and invite concentration. Maybe this is a vague, generalized way to describe his comics, but apart from their specific "abouts," I see this as the value in his work. His comics create a space to contemplate and thoughtfully look at this place. Or look at other works of fiction. Or the artists who created them.

And it's all through the lens of comics. Andrew utilizes certain aspects that are inherent to the

form, and he places them at the forefront. He really builds his stories around them. In We Are Breathing, the backbone is the page layout and his sparse, yet vibrant images, where color is a character in the story. The fact this is his early work says a lot.

Alec: I don't know you very well, but I've usually viewed you as the type of creative person who likes to leave projects in dresser drawers. Or, you'll likely complete something and quickly move on, with little sight in the rearview. What was it like compiling this collection of earlier work? What's the motive to assemble this, and why do so right now? Maybe I've been incorrect in my assumption.

Andrew: No, I think you're right. As we're talking, I have a handful of complete or near-complete projects with no immediate plans to publish them, and once a comic is printed I don't spend much time thinking about it, or looking at it, or promoting it.

But that does mean the work can be more easily forgotten, both by myself and by readers. So with that in mind, I'm collecting old work because I want people to see it and because I want to see it again myself. I wanted to reflect on these comics, the fact that I made them, and how they do or don't hold up to my critical and aesthetic standards now. I wanted to see how the ideas in them fit together. I like the idea of holding a book in my hands that contains years of my life.

Reading this collection, I was reminded of the fact that you have been making comics for quite a while. I became aware of you in maybe 2011 or 2012, when some of the work collected here started to appear. And I believe you were creating comics before that, too. That's more than a decade as a maker in this art form.

People come and go in comics, and people stay and stick with comics. I'm interested in your commitment to this thing. More so than regularly making new work, it seems like a practice for you. Maybe it's meditative, which some of the work collected here seems to reflect.

I've been thinking about this a lot lately. I suppose that's another motivation for putting together a collection. As you know, one of my main projects has become an annual comic called Yearly, which I've committed at least notionally to publishing once a year until I die. So I've made the Idea of sticking to comics a core part of my creative practice. In some ways that was a natural choice, but in other ways, it's something I actively pursued because as you say I'm well aware that people often come and go in this world. I understand why that happens; for instance, sometimes a person's life situation just doesn't allow them to devote the many, often unpaid hours to comics that it requires, but I've always admired the folks who found a way to stick with it despite the general lack of any tangible rewards. I hope to be like that myself.

Sticking with comics is also more under my control than whether I make good work. Or at least it can seem that way. In other words, I

might not know whether I'm making comics that connect with people, or whether I'm improving from one project to the next. But I can decide today, or tomorrow, or in ten years to keep drawing pages. There's comfort in that.

Beyond that, it's very simple. I love making comics. It's the only art form that has ever interested me as a creator. I like drawing. I like telling stories. One of my greatest pleasures is working through, and hopefully solving, some challenge or weakness in a comic. You said something along these lines to me recently, so maybe I'm borrowing your words. but I like the mental exercise of that problem solving, the ability to retreat into myself with ideas that stimulate me. I wouldn't get to enjoy that if I stopped making new work.

I'm also aware that my continued enthusiasm for comics is in part a function of my privilege and background. I've never been forced to take an art-related day job that might sap my energy or enthusiasm for drawing on my own time. I'm a straight white dude at no risk of quitting comics because I'm harassed or otherwise made to feel unwanted.

Your comics could be considered abstract in their appearance and function, but ultimately they seem committed to narrative. They find moments or fractures in the story to anchor to and report from, and sometimes the point of view feels fleeting or ethereal, maybe even of a spirit. Your drawings and panels reflect this. They are clear in what they are (sometimes), yet they can feel more like atmosphere than literal depiction, at times.

This approach isn't for everyone, but you're committed to it, and you've built your work around it.

I was thinking about it last night. I feel like books, drawings, songs, etc. attract their audiences because they're ultimately giving something to those that experience them, whether information, a sense of connection, intellectual stimulation, something pretty, something loud. What I described above is why I like your comics. It's a chance to look at storytelling another way. Is there a similar feeling for you when making them? Or do stories just present themselves to you in this way?

It's only one piece of your question, but I'm happy that you noticed the balance between abstraction and narrative because I've been chasing that for a long time. I love stories, but I also love drawings that just function as mark-making. Those two worlds don't always intersect, but with comics I think they fit together naturally. Think, for example, of the way that some panels in even the most traditional narrative comic might look completely abstract when considered individually. A ball zooming across a field in a sports manga. An explosion of dust and stars in a newspaper strip. A chiaroscuro figure barely visible in a sea of black ink. Images like that fascinate and compel me, so I want to make work that pushes even further in that direction, creating abstract sequences that have narrative resonance because of the context in which they appear.

I do feel like some of the pieces in this collection use abstraction or tone as a crutch. I create an atmosphere where readers assume a lack of clarity in the story or in what a drawing depicts is purposeful — when in fact I wanted that story or that image to be perfectly clear, but my skills just weren't up to the task! So I'm working to improve on that front, and ensure the moments of mystery are intentional.

In terms of whether this approach to storytelling comes naturally to me, I sometimes think about the poet Paul Valery, who supposedly said that he couldn't write fiction because he couldn't bear to write sentences like, "The marquise went out at five o'clock." Like most good quotes, this can be interpreted a number of ways, but to me, it means that constructing straightforward narrative works can often feel like a chore to me and so it probably won't be compelling to my readers. Plus, Valery's objection is even more true if you have to draw the marquise going out in addition to writing it!

I have sometimes tried to create more narrative work, but it tends to either collapse under the weight of accumulated plot points or become more ephemeral and poetic over time as I refine it. So I might imagine a story where the marquise does have to go out at five, but then I wonder — could that perhaps be implied instead of depicted? Could a sequence where the marquise goes out be more concerned with the rhythm of his life or with the feeling of stepping out into a sharply cold evening than with the simple communication of factual information? My interests are often pulled in that direction. But I also want to be kind to my readers by providing some amount of narrative, some straightforward statements of fact to allow folks a path into the work.

Describing my preferred point of view in storytelling as ethereal is another good insight. A number of my comics, both in this collection and in more recent work, have even featured ghosts or ghostly figures. I suppose ghosts are a good window into some of the themes that interest me — time, death, memory — and I also love the idea of a ghost, a presence, that hovers just behind your shoulder in quiet observation. Placing the reader in that position creates a sense of intimacy that I often want to cultivate in my work. Second person narration, which also appears in a few of these comics, can help create that same feeling.

Do you consider the reader much? I feel like you do, but some of the comics in this collection, mostly the one-off meditations or short poetry pieces, feel more concerned with whatever you were experiencing in the time you made them. They seem more for you, and they're a bit spontaneous (seemingly). I'm curious how you approached that type of work at the time you made it, as well as how you view it now.

I'm certainly thinking about the reader in terms of clarity, going back to what I mentioned previously about wanting to be more intentional regarding what parts of my stories are clear versus left mysterious. I suppose truly self-indulgent work wouldn't be concerned with that. Plus, of course, I do publish the work. So I want people to read it.

But some cartoonists talk about imagining an ideal reader, or even writing for a specific person, and I don't often have that in mind. I think all the work is for me at the end of the day.

While I feel true, immeasurable gratitude for anyone who reads my comics, let alone anyone who lets me know that they've enjoyed my work, I often derive the most satisfaction from my own sense of whether or not a piece has succeeded.

In terms of the short poetry pieces, especially the ones that appear in this collection, it's true that they're often more spontaneous and less considered. For example, the one-page strips I've chosen to include here are culled from a much larger selection of work that I was posting online from about 2012 to 2015. Hundreds of strips. The best of them are good, the worst of them are clumsy, and a significant portion is mediocre and repetitive. I improved from churning out that work, of course, and sometimes I did stumble upon making a good strip, but it also encouraged (or maybe formed) a habit of, at times, working too quickly and without enough consideration.

So I'm at a stage now where I want to tackle that kind of short, poetic work more carefully and push it to the next level of quality. Hopefully, I can manage to do that without losing the poetry or spontaneity of a strip that is drawn quickly.

With some of the earlier work in here, you were just coming out of Frank Santoro's cartoonist correspondence course, and maybe you were applying some of the lessons learned in it to your practice. I know you made comics before his class but was that a major shift for you? If so, how? And does that experience still have any direct influence in the way you make things?

I took the second iteration of Frank's correspondence course in spring 2012 and drew all but the first comic in this collection after that time. I remember Connor Willumsen was in the same running of the course, and maybe Tyler Landry, too? Then, from 2012 to about 2015, I made one-page comics for Comics Workbook and was involved in other aspects of that project, such as co-editing the 10 print issues of Comics Workbook Magazine with Zach Mason. Frank was incredibly encouraging to me during that period, when I was very unsure of myself and the value of my work. That was very kind, and I'll always appreciate it. We're still good friends now, and he continues to be very generous with his time and advice.

I'd also be remiss if I didn't mention the comics friends I made through my association with Comics Workbook and who also influenced my work — people like Sal Ingram, Madeleine Jubilee Saito, and Samuel Ombiri. Juan Fernandez is another friend I met at that period who has now channeled some of the ideas from Frank's course into his own teaching practice. I'm excited to see where that goes.

However, it does seem to me that some folks have made a parlor game out of guessing which cartoonists have taken Frank's course and/or assume that any cartoonists who have taken the course continue to approach comics with Frank's method as their primary influence.

I'll admit that does bother me a bit; it seems like a lazy critical perspective. Maybe people do this because Frank's viewpoint is so publicly articulated and so specific in some of its precepts (Grids! Work in layers of color! Draw at 100%!) that it can be tempting to assume any comics with some of those visual elements are following Frank's example. I'm sure the course was an influence on most or all of the people who took it, but I'm also sure that each of those cartoonists has a varied and complex set of influences as well as their own unique perspective.

Yeah, definitely. That makes sense. I feel like comparisons are a good shorthand for a quick description or pitch, but they don't explain nuance or why very well. The comparison point can overshadow what's actually on display, too. Do you feel your participation in Frank's course has informed how people have decided to see your work? Has it limited the perception of it?

I hope not! That's not for me to say, I guess.

Of course, I don't have a problem with citing stylistic comparisons or possible influences as one lens for talking about a comic. I would certainly be happy to have my work compared to Frank's because he's a great cartoonist. He would be an influence even if I'd never taken his course.

Reading "While A Soft Fog Wanders", the story echoes what you said above, about individual panels appearing abstract when removed from their context. But you make that the point of the story, in a way.

Individual scenes transpire per panel as the action referred to in the title (a soft fog wandering) occurs, and some of those scenes continue in subsequent panels, but the story mostly revolves around isolated shots. You, or an omniscient narrator, show us individual, seemingly unrelated images, yet that same narrator conjures an interaction between these images, to create something larger.

I'm interested in how you view perspective in comics, as a tool, and as an underlying force. I don't mean to be mystical about it, but that story, specifically, gets at something beyond a person's ordinary ability to see. And comics tow a weird line in terms of story POV. Do you think comics can show us something about, not necessarily individual perspectives, but perspective itself?

There's definitely a mysticism to the process of comics like Soft Fog, just because it can feel a little magical when a comic like that works right. I generate images that feel compelling or linked to me for whatever reason and then place them in a sequence that seems correct. It's difficult to talk about because the process of deciding how to sequence those images is very intuitive, but I also think about it very carefully — reordering panels many times, removing, or redrawing images, etc. When I made Soft Fog, I'm not sure I could have told you what it was "about." I certainly couldn't say now, but that comic and others like it feel successful when they evoke a consistent mood. A fuzzy feeling at the back of your neck or in the corner of your mind.

On perspective, I've always enjoyed the way that

comics can jump from scene to scene, image to image, in a way that, at least for me, can feel more natural than say a montage in film. Of course, many people have talked about how this reflects the way our memories work, but I'd go farther and say this is often how my brain works in general. Jumping from one thought to the next, making connections that are hard to retrace once a few seconds have passed. I enjoy trying to replicate that in comics.

What do you want from a comic when you read it? What can a great comic do?

At this point, I'm always reading comics as a cartoonist on some level — looking for tricks I can steal, noticing tiny details in the printing quality, thinking about how I might change the comic if it was my own work.

This can be frustrating because it risks taking me out of the reading experience. But it also means I'm just as likely to have my breath taken away by a scribbled shadow as by some masterful moment in the storytelling. That range just doesn't exist for me in any other medium. In prose, which I also love, I might come across a beautiful sentence, but for me, that's not the same microscopic encapsulation of the creator's worldview as a quickly dashed off but perfect drawing in the corner of some panel.

So I suppose that's what I'm looking for in a comic: an experience where the many, nested levels of art and writing and design and craft that go into the work are perfectly interacting, speaking to each other and creating something unique.

Another way of describing this is to say that when I read work by a great cartoonist, I sometimes have the strange and wonderful experience of going out into the world and being able to picture what I'm seeing as if that cartoonist had drawn it. It never lasts long. But it's always really lovely.

When adapting another's work, do you simply apply how you see the world to it? Or, are you trying to find out more about that particular author's lens? In this collection, you adapt a short story by Italo Calvino titled "A Beautiful March Day". I want to say it's one of the very few times you've depicted violence at all, let alone so directly. That violence is inherent to the story you adapted, but you decided how to present it and executed that. It's an interesting place for you and Calvino to meet.

It's interesting to reflect on that story, which I included because it's the earliest piece of my work that I can look at today without completely cringing. With that in mind, I'm sure it isn't a coincidence that I see in that comic the seeds of several threads that are still important to my work today.

I still enjoy adaptation — or perhaps appropriation, in some cases — and the process of condensing, cutting up, and even resequencing text written by someone else is an exciting challenge. I suppose I am trying to understand the author better and use their lens as a way of pushing my work to new places. But I'm also trying to accentuate certain elements of their work; a sense of mood or place, for example, that might be present in the original piece but better emphasized using comics.

I should also mention Calvino has remained an important influence for, among other reasons, his ability to write short stories that succeed individually but work together to create a broader narrative. Plus, it's funny to me that this is an adaptation three or four levels deep — from an actual historical event, to historical accounts of that event, to Shakespeare, to Calvino, to me. I included a few snippets of dialogue from Shakespeare as a nod to that fact, I hope more to poke fun at myself than to be pretentious.

Your point about violence is perceptive — you're right, of course, but that hadn't occurred to me. My first thought is that this might be related to my disinterest in traditional approaches to storytelling, which we've already discussed. Violence is so often inherent to our conception of what "conflict" means, in a narrative context, and maybe I've tended to avoid it as a result.

Yeah. Or, violence is an idea that's uninteresting to you. Which is totally fine. That said, I could see your comics distilling and depicting violence or violent events effectively. I think you could present violence in a way that impresses upon a reader in a different way, that maybe dissects it or observes it from another vantage point. Excuse me for trying to pawn ideas on you. I guess I just want to see your version of a fistfight, haha.

Are there other ideas, themes, threads, or approaches that are featured in this collection that you believe you're still exploring? Adaptation is one example. But what else? Of those ideas, what has telling stories about them taught you of these concepts? Or, has your work only presented you with more questions?

I'm still interested in second-person narration and in finding other tools that create a sense of intimacy and connection between myself and the reader. I'm still trying to make work that has some completely abstract and other fully narrative sequences, and that thrives in the space between those worlds. I still spend a lot of time thinking about time and memory. I will always love to draw trees and water and wispy clouds.

On the other hand, I do think I've left behind the approach of Soft Fog or some of the Comics Workbook strips, where very loosely related images hint at some tone or theme. That approach may appear in portions of my comics going forward, but it's not enough to carry a project by itself.

I also think I'm less attached to formalism and constraints than I once was. I'm more aware of the complexities and the nested levels of problem-solving that must be brought to bear to make a good comic. As a result, I'm often more impressed — in my own work and in the work I read — with subtlety than with some "clever," formal trick. Though I do have a soft spot for that stuff. I identify quite a bit with a Dash Shaw interview from many years ago, where he describes himself as "annoyingly a formalist."

I feel the same way, in that I can't help but be drawn to some degree of formalism.

I think one evolution that starts to appear in the last few comics in this collection, and that I'm still grappling with today, is my desire to come to some conclusion, however small, about these ideas that I'm working through, again and again.

In other words, I've come to feel that an important goal with many of my comics is to have a happy ending: not trite, superficial happiness, but a happiness that comes from grappling with difficult ideas and arriving at some truth, some insight.

Perhaps "satisfying" (or, an ending that does not lean on the narrative tropes around satisfaction or resolution) is a better way of describing it.

bibliography

Solo Work (Print)

Consumed (self-published, 2011)

Sexbuzz (self-published, 2012)

Territory (self-published, 2012)

Comics Workbook #1 (Comics Workbook, 2013)

We Will Remain (Retrofit Comics, 2013)

Comics Workbook #2:
Variations/Deconstructions
(Comics Workbook, 2013)

Tides (self-published, 2013)

Black Pillars #1-2 (self-published, 2013-2014)

While a Soft Fog Wanders (self-published, 2014)

My Name Is Martin Shears (self-published, 2014)

Fill'd/Empty'd (self-published by Warren
Craghead, 2014)

Those Goddamn Fuckers (Uncivilized Books,
2015, written by Alec Berry)

Ley Lines: For Lives (Czap Books & Grindstone
Comics, 2015)

Dark Light/I Raised an Arm (self-published by
Warren Craghead, 2015)

M (self-published, 2015)

Muscle Memory (self-published, 2016, with
Kimball Anderson)

Read & Erase (self-published, 2016)

N (self-published, 2017)

All There Is (self-published, 2017)

Things As They Were (self-published, 2018)

Ways to Survive in the Wilderness (self-
published, 2021)

Letters I'll Send Tomorrow (self-published, 2021)

Yearly 2018-2021 (self-published)

Anthology Contributions

Rebus (2014)

Double Nickels Forever (2014)

Inactions Comics 1: Productivity (2015)

Over the Line: An Introduction to Poetry Comics (2015)

Warmer: A Collection of Comics About Climate Change for the Fearful and Hopeful (2017)

Inkbrick 8 (2018)

Inkbrick 10 (2019)

Rust Best Review Vol 3 (2021)